NELSON'S N WEST INDIA READERS 5

NELSON'S NEW WEST INDIAN READERS 5

CLIVE BORELY

UNIVERSITY PRESS

UNIVERSITY PRESS

Great Clarendon Street, Oxford, OX2 6DP, United Kingdom

Oxford University Press is a department of the University of Oxford.
It furthers the University's objective of excellence in research, scholarship,
and education by publishing worldwide. Oxford is a registered trade mark of
Oxford University Press in the UK and in certain other countries

Text © Clive Borely 1984
Original illustrations © Oxford University Press 2014

The moral rights of the authors have been asserted

First published by Thomas Nelson and Sons Ltd in 1984
This edition published by Oxford University Press in 2014

All rights reserved. No part of this publication may be reproduced,
stored in a retrieval system, or transmitted, in any form or by any
means, without the prior permission in writing of Oxford University
Press, or as expressly permitted by law, by licence or under terms
agreed with the appropriate reprographics rights organization.
Enquiries concerning reproduction outside the scope of the above
should be sent to the Rights Department, Oxford University Press, at
the address above.

You must not circulate this work in any other form and you must
impose this same condition on any acquirer

British Library Cataloguing in Publication Data
Data available

978-0-1756-6330-9

10 9 8 7 6 5 4 3 2

Printed by Multivista Global Ltd.

Although we have made every effort to trace and contact all
copyright holders before publication this has not been possible in all
cases. If notified, the publisher will rectify any errors or omissions at
the earliest opportunity.

Links to third party websites are provided by Oxford in good faith
and for information only. Oxford disclaims any responsibility for
the materials contained in any third party website referenced in
this work.

Contents

	Acknowledgements	6
	To the Teacher	7
1.	The Hummingbird and the Hibiscus	9
2.	Anancy	13
3.	The Valley of the Hawk	15
4.	Night of the Shango	17
5.	Preparations for the Hunt	18
6.	Hot Bakes and Chocolate	24
7.	Ysassi – Defender of Jamaica	31
8.	A Search for Tracks	34
9.	The Arawak's Story	39
10.	Mr Wheeler	43
	The story of how Anansi acquired his limp	
11.	Noise	51
12.	North and South	52
13.	Examinations	54
14.	The Quarrel	64
15.	The Master Sisserou of Dominica	66
16.	Theophilus Albert Marryshow	77
17.	The Master Kite	81
18.	The Incas of Peru	87
19.	The West Indian String of Pearls	94
20.	Humming Bird Makes It	96
21.	Marcus Garvey	103
22.	Market Women	110
23.	A Piper	112
24.	An Exciting Test Match	113
25.	Learie Constantine	119
26.	Port Royal – City of Silence	124
27.	June	131
28.	Ra II Arrives in Barbados	132
29.	A Sad Song about Greenwich Village	141
30.	Jamaica Market	142
31.	A Great Fast Bowler	144
32.	What? Protect a Hawk?	152

Acknowledgements

Clive Borely and the publishers are grateful to the following for permission to use copyright material in this book:

Mrs Zena Moore for *The Incas of Peru*; Patricia Lalla-Aquing for *Preparations for the Hunt*; Hollis Knight for *Hot Bakes and Chocolate* from IN AND OUT OF SCHOOL and *An Exciting Test Match*; Alma Norman for *Ysassi—Defender of Jamaica*; Oxford University Press and Sir Philip Sherlock for *Mr Wheeler—The Story of how Anansi acquired his Limp* from WEST INDIAN FOLK-TALES; Michael Joseph Ltd and Eleanor Farjeon for *The Quarrel* from SILVER SAND AND SNOW; Wm Collins and Sangster Limited in association with the Ministry of Education, for the extract *Examinations* from SPRAT MORRISON by Jean Da Costa; Longman and Thérèse Mills for *Theophilus Albert Marryshow* and *Marcus Garvey* from GREAT WEST INDIANS; Mrs Daisy Myrie for *Market Women*; Harold La Borde for the extract *Humming Bird Makes It* from AN OCEAN TO OURSELVES published by Longman; UNESCO Features for *Port Royal — City of Silence*; Miss Agnes Maxwell-Hall for *Jamaica Market*; Harold M Telemaque for *June*; André Deutsch Limited for *What? Protect a Hawk?* from BABA AND MR BIG by C. Everard Palmer; C. L. R. James and Hutchinson Publishing Group Limited for *A Great Fast Bowler* from BEYOND A BOUNDARY by C. L. R. James; Mrs Undine Giuseppi for *Learie Constantine* from A LOOK AT LEARIE CONSTANTINE; George Allen and Unwin (Publishers) Ltd for *Ra II Arrives in Barbados* from RA II by Thor Heyerdahl; *North and South* by Claude McKay from SELECTED POEMS OF CLAUDE MCKAY: copyright 1953 by Twayne Publishers, Inc. and reprinted with permission of Twayne Publishers, a Division of G. K. Hall & Co., Boston; André Deutsch and Michael Anthony; Terry Bett for *The Hummingbird and the Hibiscus;* Lilla Stirling for the extract form *The Upturned Turtles;* Michael Anthony for the extract from *Bright Road to El Dorado;* Ria Mercado for *The Master Sisseron of Dominica;* The New Yorker for *A Sad Song about Greenwich Village;* Lennox Honychurch for *Valley of the Hawk;* Andrew Salkey for *Anancy*.

The author and publishers wish to thank the following for permission to use photographs and illustrations included in this book:

The John Hillelson Agency Ltd: page 65
The Mansell Collection: page 124
Camera Press Ltd: page 122
Thor Heyerdahl: pages 132 and 135
Harold La Borde: pages 97 and 101
Mark Edwards: page 111
Bruce Coleman: page 53

The publishers have made every effort to make the list of acknowledgements complete, but in some cases all efforts to trace the owners of the copyright failed. It is hoped that any such omissions from the list will be excused.

Illustrated by Trevor Parkin and Maggie Ling.

To the Teacher

This is the final book in the *Nelson's New West Indian Readers* series. Like the previous ones, it presents reading material derived from a wide range of sources. The historical pieces and the stories of local heroes are intended to generate a pride in our heritage to inspire our children to greater effort and achievement. The poetry and excerpts from literature are intended to develop a sense of pleasure in reading and a desire to read more of the works of the selected authors as well as others.

The questions at the end of each prose chapter are intended primarily for class discussions and not as tests of comprehension.

It is hoped that teachers will assist their children by providing them with additional material of the appropriate reading level and subject matter to enable them to practise their reading skills and derive enjoyment and profit from so doing.

C.B.

To Thérèse and David

1 The Humming-bird and the Hibiscus

The hibiscus is a beautiful flower found in the sunny islands of the Caribbean. There are hibiscuses that are as white as the puffy clouds in the sky, others yellow as the morning sunshine sneaking through the window, some are pink as the flamingo and there are bold red ones, bright as the scarlet ibis. Then there are the shy ones who are never sure what colour they want to be—soft pastels—almost pink, almost peach, but never bold enough to be one thing or the other.

But whether bold or shy, the hibiscuses always open their petals wide and inviting. From the centre of the spreading petals a long pistil waves—a saucy feather from a lady's hat.

The beautiful hibiscuses bloom only for a day. In the morning when you awake, there they are beautiful and smiling. Sometimes there are little drops of dew shining on the petals. But when the orange sun sets in the evening, the spreading petals close tightly so they look limp. The next day you see them faded and scattered on the ground.

But it was not always so. The beauty of the hibiscus once lasted for days. The tiny humming-bird would come day after day to sip the cool nectar inside the lovely flower. One day, however a change came over the flower, that is the beginning of the story of the hibiscus and the humming-bird.

The tiny humming-bird loved to play among the flowers but his favourite was the hibiscus. The little bird would hover around the flower poking in his long beak and sipping the cool nectar from deep inside. The hibiscus would always spread its petals wider when it heard him coming. The flower always knew when he was coming. It could hear his deep hum and seen the sun reflecting off his bright colours.

Humming-bird never stayed long. He would sip quickly then dart here and there, returning from time to time. All this was very fine with the hibiscus, at first. The humming-bird was not its only visitor. The butterflies came by and it could hear their tiny voices whispering "Is it not beautiful? It lights up the forest with its colour."

The bees came to visit and the hibiscus heard them buzzing to each other. "It is so lovely. Its petals seem to smile at us."

The children came too and picked it to take to their teacher. ."This is the prettiest flower in the forest," they said.

So each day as the hibiscus heard these praises it became more and more proud of its beauty until, sad to say, it became quite vain.

Now when it heard the little humming-bird coming it would toss its head and say, "Here comes that pest again, always bothering me. I wish he would find some other flower to drink from." When humming-bird tried to take a sip of the nectar, the hibiscus closed its petals and shook itself angrily.

"Why, what's the matter, my friend," asked humming-bird in his deep voice. "Are you all right?" He was concerned for his friend.

"I am very well," replied the flower, "but I would be better if you would stop poking at me with your sharp beak. Don't you know that I am the most beautiful flower in the forest? Everyone says so. Your sharp beak may scratch me and spoil my beauty. Go find another flower to drink from."

"Have I ever hurt you my friend?" asked the little bird sadly. "I have always been tender and gentle. I have never taken more than I needed of your sweet nectar."

"That was when I was an ordinary flower. Now I am the prettiest flower in the forest I must be more careful.

Fly away and bother someone else."

The little humming-bird flew away sadly. Even his hum was softer now. "What shall I do?" he thought. "I always drank from the hibiscus. Will any of the other flowers let me sip from them? Maybe they will chase me away. But I must live somehow."

So off he flew and asked the other flowers. The yellow-bell invited him in. The mango blossoms said, "Have your fill." As the days went by and the other flowers heard his story they called to him and invited him to drink. The little bird was grateful to the other flowers but somehow their nectar was not as sweet as that of the hibiscus. He missed it very much. He never went near it now. But he could see its lovely face as he flew by. At night when he sat on his roost he thought of it so much it made him sad, for he loved the beautiful flower.

Soon everyone could see his sadness. His colours seemed to fade. He no longer looked like a jewel flashing in the sun. The bees buzzed about it and the flowers shook their heads sorrowfully. Everyone was sorry for the little bird.

Then somehow his story reached the ears of the Queen of the Flowers. "I shall put an end to this," she said. "The little bird shall suffer no more and the vain hibiscus must be taught a lesson." And so she sent her butterfly messengers to the hibiscus with these words: "Your beauty has made you vain and selfish. You must learn that loving and sharing are also beautiful. Send for the little bird and tell him to come and drink your nectar once more. So that you may never forget this lesson your punishment will be this. Your beauty will only last a day. Every morning a new flower will bloom, only to fade with the setting sun."

Next time you see the hibiscus folding its petals at sunset, remember this story.

TERRY BETT

1 What do you think is the moral of the story of the hibiscus?
2 Do you know another story that tries to teach us a lesson?
3 Make up a story to teach little children to be kind to old people.

2 Anancy

Anancy is a spider;
Anancy is a man;
Anancy's West Indian
And West African.

Sometimes, he wears a waistcoat;
Sometimes, he carries a cane;
Sometimes, he sports a top hat;
Sometimes, he's just a plain,
Ordinary, black, hairy spider.

Anancy is vastly cunning,
Tremendously greedy,
Excessively charming,
Hopelessly dishonest,
Warmly loving,
Firmly confident,
Fiercely wild,
A fabulous character,
Completely out of our mind
And out of his, too.

Anancy is a master planner,
A great user
Of other people's plans;
He pockets everybody's food,
Shelter, land, money, and more;
He achieves mountains of things,
Like stolen flour dumplings;
He deceives millions of people,
Even the man in the moon;
And he solves all the mysteries
On earth, in air, under sea.

And always,
Anancy changes
From a spider into a man
And from a man into a spider
And back again
At the drop of a sleepy eyelid.

       ANDREW SALKEY *(Jamaica)*

(There are two spellings of *Anancy*, both are accepted.)

3 Valley of the Hawk

Look up to the call
Where the hawk soars
In lazy turns on unseen spirals
Of a barren sky.
A winged dot of freedom
Wheeling in a wilderness of silence,
Taunting the youth
Who seeking solitude has climbed
Through the gateway of the hills
Above the mirror of the sea.

Look up to the call
Lost in eclipse against the sun,
Screaming through the virgin blue
Between the verdant frame
Towards the crowded glitter dust,
The shining city rooftops
Clinging to the coast.
And the youth follows the fall
With eyes that speed on downwards
To the Babylon he left behind
All washed, lashed, lapped
By silver waves, a line of sequins
Breaking gently on a cluttered shore.

Look up to the call
Reeling still above the deep womb
Of this blue valley
Draped in morning mist
And lingering dew on silent palm leaves,
On petals of the flamingo immortelles
Where birds sip nectar cupped in scarlet.

The naked body dips,
Dives through liquid emerald
Rises in a muscled arc,
A boy shaking cold diamonds
From his hair.

This is the valley
Of the hawk and the youth
And his secret shelter
Lost between the peaks
Of tranquillity and quietude.
Where twisting charcoal smoke
Climbs through the morning sun,
Unfolding skywards to the call
Beyond the green
And blue
And purple walls
Of this volcanic cul-de-sac.

LENNOX HONYCHURCH *(Dominica)*

4 Night of the Shango

From Mayaro to Port of Spain
Los Iros to La Romain
They come! To the night of the SHANGO.

The drums are throbbing a wearied note
The priest is tying the frightened goat
They come! To the night of the SHANGO.

The night is dark, frightened dogs bark
Doctor, limey and city clerk
They come! To the night of the SHANGO.

Some are walking the dreary mile
Through the forest in single file
They come! To the night of the SHANGO.

Young and old with faces bold
Children shivering in the cold
Yet they come! To the night of the SHANGO!

The moon is peeping through the trees
The gods are dancing in the leaves
Tonight is the night of the SHANGO!

MILTON SCOBIE

5 Preparations for the Hunt

As the sun crept slowly over the Eastern sky, casting a rosy glow on the trees and hilltops, a little Arawak boy sprung out of his cotton hammock, leapt over several low wooden stools, edged past his father's hammock, and crept out through the back of the ajoupa. He raced down to the centre of the village and, when he reached the priest-hut, stopped. He looked around expectantly at the neat circle of ajoupas which surrounded him. All of them looked alike with their thatched roofs reaching low, almost touching the ground. No human sound was audible—only the screeching of an owl and the low hooting of some jungle bird. He waited. Still no sign of anyone. Quickly he put his fingers to his mouth and let out a long, shrill whistle. Seconds later he got his first reply—one whistle, then another, and then several more. He knew now that his friends were awake and would come to meet him.

Today was a special day for Namba and his friends. It was the day that the hunting party left, and it was their task to help in the preparations. When the men left the village they were practically in charge. They had to help protect the women and girls and see that everything went well. They felt proud to be given such responsibilities, Namba especially, since he was the oldest among the boys. He walked into the priest-hut and looked around. He felt a special joy this morning, for, with each hunt that took place, his chances of joining it grew increasingly greater.

"Namba!"

Namba snapped out of his daydream. It was one of

his friends who was calling him. The boy, much younger than Namba himself, staggered into the hut under the weight of too many wooden arrows and bone-tipped spears, and a basket which probably contained meat or fish cured with herbs and some coarse bread made from cassava which had been pounded in a wooden mortar. Namba helped him to unload it in a corner of the hut. Soon two more children came, bringing with them gaily-coloured feathers taken from some large macaw caught on the last hunting trip, and a calabash gourd filled with red *roucou* or anatto dye. The men painted their bodies with the dye to protect them from the heat of the sun and to scare their enemies off.

And so most of the children came. Then came the women bringing more foodstuffs with them. Finally the men came—about twenty of them—with an assortment of hunting equipment and a few fierce-looking dumb dogs.

By this time everybody was seated in an orderly fashion inside the hut. Namba's father was in front of the Cacique's throne, rubbing two pieces of stone together in a heap of straw in order to catch fire to it. The priest, on the other hand, sat with his legs folded under him. He was wearing some of the huge feathers which the children had brought. His skin was painted with the red *roucou* dye. He looked very solemn indeed. The women too were well decorated with chip-chip shells, colourful wild beads, and pieces of cotton which they had woven and then dyed with fruit stains. Some of them had small pieces of gold ornaments. The hut was a colourful sight. A general air of excitement prevailed.

Soon, little wisps of smoke started to rise up from the heap of straw which was beginning to catch fire. Namba's father added some wood to keep it burning longer. This was the signal for the Cacique to arrive. He was the most important man in the village. Everybody depended on

him to settle quarrels and to make decisions. He in turn relied on the priest to advise him on the right decisions to make. Today the priest would advise him on how many men should go on the hunt, how long they should go for, or whether they should go at all.

Everyone hoped that the signs would be good.

The Cacique took out a pouch full of dried tobacco leaves. He gave it to the priest who scattered some of it over the smouldering ashes. He then placed various *zemis*, or wooden idols, around the smoking heap of tobacco leaves. With two pieces of hollow reed stuck in his nostrils, he then began to inhale the tobacco smoke. Everyone was perfectly silent. Not even the smallest baby cried. This was important, since, at any time now, the gods of the tribe would relay their messages to the tribe through the priest. All eyes were trained on the priest. Slowly he got up, walked around the *zemis*, inhaled the tobacco smoke once more, and then started to speak in a low, hoarse voice.

There was loud rejoicing at the predictions of the priest. The gods had informed him that the hunt would be successful. People began pouring out of the hut into the open courtyard. Soon there was a long line of men and women carrying supplies down to the dugouts at the river's edge. Everyone was going to say goodbye to the hunting party. Namba looked at the men as they got into the dugouts and arranged their supplies and weapons. He knew that it was necessary for them to go hunting in order to obtain meat for his people. He knew, too, how happy everyone would be when they returned with iguanas, and agoutis. There would be dancing and general feasting. He looked longingly as the canoes shoved off from the river's edge. He hoped for the day when he too would be on those canoes.

"Soon my turn will come," he thought. "Soon."

1. How did Namba know that his friends were up?
2. What special work did Namba and his friends have to do?
3. Why did all the people gather at the priest's hut? Why were they happy when the priest spoke?
4. Name some of the animals hunted by the Arawaks.
5. Draw a picture of an Arawak hunter or an Arawak woman.

6 Hot Bakes and Chocolate

As Carlton walked home that Friday afternoon, it occurred to him that he was worse off than a condemned murderer on his way to the gallows. The condemned man could at least be certain that his punishment would be swift, painless, and final.

Carlton knew that his own punishment would be neither swift nor painless nor final. His mother would flog him until she grew tired—not that she tired easily—or until Aunt Rose, her sister who lived in the front apartment, would rush in and say,

"Bertha! That's enough! What are you trying to do, kill the child?"

His mother would then allow herself to be subdued. Aunt Rose would take away the strap before more blows could be administered, and the second phase of his punishment would begin. He would be ordered to kneel in a corner and for the next hour or two he would hear nothing else but a hastily improvised and graphically illustrated sermon on the evil that was certain to befall wayward, no-good reprobates, as he was usually considered to be at times such as these. All such boys, his mother would say, must eventually face the magistrate, then the judge, and then the hangman. Or worse still, the mighty Jehovah may decide to smite the offenders instantly, so that their souls may proceed immediately to the fires of hell. This last alternative was a constant source of worry to Carlton, for proof of it once lay before his very eyes. Two days after stealing twenty dollars from his mother's purse, Chalky Greene got into difficulties while bathing at Balandra and his body was never recovered.

Something else occurred to Carlton. The third phase of his punishment would be the suspension of all his privileges. That would mean no more pocket change, no going to the cinema, no watching television at Albert's home. It would also mean . . .

"Oh no! Not that . . . Lord not that."

Carlton did not realise it but he was actually shouting.

An old lady watched him in amazement. He had suddenly realised that it would also mean being banned from taking part in the school sports next Saturday.

He was already beginning to feel the pain. His legs refused to move. He quickly propped himself up against a fence. The tears were flowing freely now.

Carlton was easily the best athlete in the school. Everybody knew that. This year, running well below full speed, he had won his heats for the hundred, two-twenty, four-forty, and eight-eighty. Not even some of the teachers could throw the cricket ball as far as he could. And a short while ago, while other boys in the post-primary class were bursting their brains over twenty decimal sums, he had been the one chosen to assist the sports master, Mr Walters, in putting the tags on the prizes.

He had even seen some of 'his' prizes. The prize for the four-forty was a beautiful flashlight which carried at least three batteries. He had flicked it on and off when Mr Walters was not looking. Even in the daylight it threw a bright beam skywards. Up to a short while ago, there was no one alive who would think that that flashlight was not going to be his.

Now it was certain to go to Charles Martin. He could see Martin now, his huge calves glistening in the sun, striding forward to receive it from the Principal's wife. He could hear the 'Ooohs' and 'Aaahs' of those stupid Standard Five girls. He could see Martin now walking away from the prize table, blowing kisses to the giggling fools, shining the flashlight on them.

There could be no hope for Carlton. He could as well go home and face the music. He found his legs again but he walked as slowly as he could. If he could not avoid the punishment, the least he could do was delay it.

As he drew near to his home, he had no difficulty in visualising the events that would soon take place.

His mother would be bending over the wash tub. She always washed on Friday afternoons. In fact, the very clothes that he was wearing would go into the tub so as to be ready for Monday morning. Her huge arms would move in a rhythm of their own, up and down the scrubbing board. At times the huge unruly tub would try to unseat itself from the box on which it rested. But one powerful arm would jerk it back into place.

On seeing him, she would enquire why he was so late from school. This question posed no real problem. Any reasonable explanation would be accepted. It was the next question that would bring the walls tumbling down.

"Did you remember to pass by Miss Doris for the sou-sou hand?"

"Yes, Ma . . .but . . . "

"But what?"

She would probably stop washing, straighten up, and stare at him in apparent disbelief.

"But what? Don't tell me she didn't give it to you?"

"The money lose. I had the envelope in my shirt pocket and this afternoon when I looked for it, it was gone."

But after the first few words his mother would no longer be listening. She would be making her way inside towards the top of the cupboard where she kept the thick, black strap. She would be saying things like,

"You mean this boy go and throw away the only money I have? The money to pay the rent and to pay the shop. You think I could tell Chin that the money lose and that is why I can't pay him?"

By this time she would have reached the strap. A new idea crossed his mind. Should he at least try to sneak inside and hide the strap before he could be questioned about the money?

He thought about this for a while but decided against this particular stratagem. His mother would be in such a rage that she would hit him with anything in sight, the mop, the broomstick, even the scrubbing board. He could not risk that. His best bet, it seemed, would be to go directly to Aunt Rose and explain the situation. She might then accompany him or at least realise that pleading for him should not on any account be delayed. She might even put in the money for him.

As he made the final turn into McCarthy Lane, Carlton picked up three stones and threw them behind his back. He didn't really believe that this would work this time. It worked quite well for minor offences such as wet shoes or torn trousers. A boy in his class had even said that it worked when he had lost five dollars. But sixty dollars? Impossible!

Another shock awaited him. All the windows of Aunt Rose's apartment were closed. She was not at home. That old lady who never went out more than three or four times a year had chosen this day to go out.

Mr Singh's two daughters were at home. They were seated in their gallery, watching and waiting as if, somehow, they knew that disaster was imminent. They would certainly hear the blows, the screams, the general commotion. And for the next few days, whenever Carlton passed in front of their home, as he had to do every day, one sister would ask the other,

"Guess who got hot bakes and chocolate on Friday?"

And they would snigger, and run inside singing, "Hot bakes and chocolate, hot bakes and chocolate."

Carlton was at the gateway now. He could see his mother bending over the tub. His world had come to an end.

"Carlton."

The voice was not his mother's but was equally authoritative. It came from the street. Carlton looked around. It was Mr Walters.

"Hello, Carlton. I had so much trouble finding this

place. You look as if you've been crying. I saw you drop this envelope this afternoon while you were helping with the prizes. I picked it up but before I could give it to you, Jean de Souza took ill and I had to rush her to hospital. Do you remember? I put it in my pocket and forgot all about it until now. It looks important."

Carlton took the envelope from Mr Walters. For the second time that day his legs failed him. He sat on the ground in the gateway.

"Carlton."

It was his mother's voice.

"But look at this boy sitting down on the ground in his school clothes! Boy, why are you so late? Did you remember to pass by Miss Doris for the sou-sou hand?"

from IN AND OUT OF SCHOOL
by HOLLIS E. KNIGHT

1 Which form of punishment would have really hurt Carlton?
2 Why couldn't Carlton ignore Chalky's death, or call it an accident?
3 Do you like or dislike Charles Martin? Was he a good athlete?
4 Carlton seems to know exactly how Charles Martin would have behaved upon receiving his prize. This may be because he had seen him receive a prize on a previous occasion. Can you think of another reason?
5 Complete this sentence: 'Carlton would not consider the Standard Five girls stupid if . . .'
6 Carlton walked slowly. Did this help him in any way?
7 Did the throwing of the three stones behind his back really help Carlton? Earlier in the story Carlton had been certain that this would not have worked. Is there a reason why he might have been thinking differently towards the end?
8 The writer suggests that Carlton's mother was a strong woman. If she were a thin, sickly person, would the story be more interesting or less interesting?

7 Ysassi – Defender of Jamaica

The English brought their soldiers, but Jamaicans
  stayed to fight.
The English had the numbers but Jamaicans had the
  right.
Ysassi said, "We'll beat them back."
Defying English might.

They slogged across the mountains, they slogged across
  the plains.
In swamps and sullen rivers, in dry times and in rains,
They battled for Jamaica
And got fever for their pains.

They're short of food and water, but still they stumble
  on.
They chase the flitting shadows, but they find the men
  are gone.
And Ysassi grimly mutters,
"We'll fight until we've won."

D'Oyley tried to crush resistance. To Ysassi he
  declared,
"If you'll come out and surrender you can go off
  anywhere.
We will offer you safe conduct."
But he answered, "I stay here."

One time he had to flee them, but he grimly said,
  "Oh, no.
I'll go back home from Cuba, to battle sure and slow,
And we'll get our own land back again
The only way I know."

High above Puerto Nuevo in the trackless
    mountainside,
Ysassi and defenders built a fort where they could hide,
And they swooped on the invaders,
Then they melted back inside.
The English stormed and took it; the defenders lost
    the fort.
D'Oyley chuckled, "Now we've beat them." But he
    laughed before he ought.
For Ysassi and de Bolas they retreated—
But they fought.

In the hidden mountain shadows, Ysassi tells his plan.
  "Will any fight for homeland and act a free-born
    man?"
The black men roared approval
and the long hard fight began.

"We haven't got an army," Ysassi grimly said,
"But we know our native mountains in this land
    where we were bred."
"We will fight," vowed Juan de Bolas,
And they followed where he led.

Black and white men fought together, both of them
    Jamaica men,
Fought the foe, but they discovered that they could
    not win again.
"No surrender," urged Ysassi.
But de Bolas went to them.

Left alone then, brave Ysassi told the remnants of his
    band,
"English soon will know our secrets. We can't make
    another stand.
After five long years of fighting
We must flee our native land."

With a heavy heart and weary did Ysassi leave this
  shore.
Watched the cliffs recede from vision, heard the
  ocean's muffled roar,
Looked his last upon his birthplace
Which he knew he'd see no more.

ALMA NORMAN

8 A Search for Tracks

Jim and Jude lay on the verandah steps and watched Bobtail the lizard scamper across the stone walk. Bobtail had lost half his long beautiful blue tail.

"I wish we could feed them," said Jim. He put a bit of cheese on the doorstep and they lay quietly watching. Very soon Bobtail came scuttling up with the pouch under his chin puffing back and forth. He scampered around the cheese, and then bit into it and instantly scurried off with it.

"Let's try it again and see how close he will come."

They waited, talking in whispers. Above them the palm leaves clicked softly. A hot breeze blew over them.

"When the rain comes down the palm trees rattle hard. It wakes you in the middle of the night. I woke up last night and the palms were rattling hard," said Jude. "I thought it was the rain but the stars were out. It was only the wind."

Just then Bobtail scooted out from under the leaf, nibbled the crumb of cheese, and scuttled off as Ma Izzy opened the door.

"Take these conch fritters to your Uncle Joie," she said.

"Ah, ma!" said Jude, "he'll keep us talking all morning."

"None of that, boy! Hurry along and when you come back there's a plate for you."

"But he's always—"

"Get going, boy," Ma Izzy slammed the door.

The boys got up slowly.

"He's always talking about his hat that he lost, or asking questions," growled Jude.

Ma Izzy sighed. "If only it would rain, before everything's ruined, we could get him a hat when we go to Nassau in the fall."

The boys trudged along the hot coral street. At Jude's knock Uncle Joie called, "Come in! Come in! Bring your friend in!"

"We'll have to go," said Jude.

But Jim saw the long net stretched across the length of the house, and stepped in. He had never been in Uncle Joie's house. He gazed in delight at the collection of curious things suspended from the enormous fish net.

Uncle Joie took the fritters. "Your mother's a nice kind woman," he said. "I see your friend likes my curiosities."

"He's never been in here before," said Jude.

Jim gaped at the dried fish, the shells and even the eggs, caught in this great long net.

"All these are Bahamian products. I caught all these fish, and found these shells. I will tell you about them—"

"We have to go," said Jude. "We have to go to the post office."

"The post office can wait," said Uncle Joie. "You boys are always hankering to go to the post office. What did you boys order in the mail catalogue?"

Jude hung his head. "Nothing," he said.

"I want to see these things," said Jim. "Wait up for a bit."

"This is a flying fish, and here's a horse fish. Here's a Spanish crayfish. Here are some of our land crabs. Here's a big sea crab. Here's a yellow-tailed fish, a dried grouper, a jack, a grunt."

Uncle Joie kept pointing. "These are some of our conch, the horse conch, the fighting conch, the flame helmet conch, the trumpet tuton, the sea biscuit, the murex."

"We must go," said Jude. He didn't want to hear Uncle Joie any longer.

"Here's a porcupine fish. Look at its bristles," said

Uncle Joie. "You've never seen anything like this, Jim."

"It has quills like a porcupine. Look Jude," said Jim.

"I've never seen a porcupine," said Jude.

"Their quills are longer and they have short legs. They can't move very fast. My dad says they don't throw their quills. My dog tried to bite one and got quills in his mouth. Is that a shark?" asked Jim.

"That's a nursing shark. He's a friendly curious fellow, not a killer."

"He's not so big," said Jim.

"He's shrunk. He was eight feet when I caught him," said Uncle Joie.

"What kind of an egg is that?" asked Jim.

"That's a turtle egg. I found a turtle's nest in the sand on one of the outer cays. It had 165 eggs. I saved that one for a souvenir. I blew out the contents. That other one is a turtle egg I found in a hole dug by a turtle two yards deep. It had 99 eggs."

"My father says that if people take the eggs from the turtles there won't be any turtles any more," said Jim.

"Yes, that's true," said Uncle Joie, "but those were the days when we got little money for our fish and we did need eggs for a change. We took them around and shared them with our neighbours. There were no bicycles or refrigerators on the island in those days."

"There's an old turtle that lays her eggs in about the same place in the North Cay, at the other end of the island, about this time. The boys look for her tracks, and usually get them before they spoil."

"Did anyone ever see her lay her eggs?" asked Jim.

"Not that I know of," said Uncle Joie.

"Now that is a gull egg. That year we went around the Cays in Exuma and got 85 dozen gull eggs. It was fun hunting them. They lay their eggs in the hollows of the coral that are filled with sand, under some scrubby bushes."

"Do they sit on these like Annie Bell's cluckers?"

Jude was getting more impatient.

"Oh no, they drop their eggs and fly away. After a while they'd come back and lay another one. When we found a nest we'd throw the eggs into the sea and come back next day and there would be a collection of fresh eggs dropped in about the same place."

"Then there wouldn't be any gull babies," said Jude.

"Oh, there were always some we didn't find. They usually found a spot under the bushes that we didn't catch."

"We have to go," said Jude for the third time. "Ma has conch fritters for us."

"I forgot about the fritters!" Jim raced to the door.

"Goodbye, Uncle Joie," they called.

1 Do you know anybody like Uncle Joie?
2 Describe a visit to an old relation or friend who has a lot of interesting things to show or talk about.
3 Try to find out about the laying habits of turtles in your country.
4 There are many people who are trying to save the turtles from extinction. Find out what you can do to help.

9 The Arawak's Story

During the sixteenth century, the British and the Spanish fought several battles for possession of the West Indian islands. This story tells of the reaction of some of the Indians to one such attack.

Before Ayun left for his canoe he walked back to the place of the huts. He went directly to the hut in the centre and although it was pitch black he knew exactly where Arama's hammock was. For his own was beside it. When the elderly one heard the footsteps, he said: "Where is the Spaniard?"

"He is on the beach. Oh, now he is gone to the Spanish hut."

"You saw the ship?"

"Yes. From the start. It came nearer in. It is the English. I promised the Spaniard that I was going out to it."

"To tell them to go away?"

"To tell them to land," Ayun smiled in the dark. "I told the Spaniard we had one thousand armed men in the marshes and now he is anxious for the English to land."

"Anxious?" The old man turned.

"For us to kill them. For them to die."

Arama said sadly, "I always help the sea-people to live."

"Yes, and they always help us to die." Ayun felt his blood growing warm. "And they fight our brothers in the north. And often they destroy their villages. They preserve Chacomaray, yes, because we supply the food and the water."

"Because I made it so." The old man rose to a sitting position. Ayun just heard the creak of the hammock. "Because I made it so, Fierce One. Because I help everybody."

39

"And because you made it so, the Spaniard threatened to destroy our village. Did you hear him?" Then he changed from the Arawak tongue and broke into Spanish, mimicking Don Ricardo: "'Cacique, I will not again draw this sword without staining it with blood. If you let them land we destroy the village.'" Then in the dark his Arawak words gushed like the hiss of a viper: "I am going to the English to tell them to land. There will not be much fighting because there are just ten Spaniards."

"And the thousand warriors?" Arama looked towards him in the dark. Ayun laughed. Then he suddenly felt what must have passed through Arama's mind, and he himself was seized with fear. For what would happen after the English had slaughtered the ten Spaniards? Who would deal with them then? For one thing he did not know how many men the English had and what weapons they had brought. After they had killed the Spaniards it was quite likely they would seek to destroy the Arawaks. For all the sea-people were blood-thirsty. He did not want an open fight until he knew how many men they had. In fact he did not want an open fight at all, for it meant that whatever happened many Arawaks would die. And die for what? He wanted the sea-people to destroy each other.

The old man was still waiting for an answer about the thousand warriors. For he did not know if Ayun had armed them and had them waiting. But he heard no war-chants and shrieks and now he realised what Ayun's laughter had meant. He said calmly, "You are going to the English ship. If it is Dudley—?"

"Dudley? Dudley will not come back. He was awaiting Guatteral and now he is already gone. He spoke of catching the Trade Winds."

In the dark the old man was silent and wistful. He had been sitting up, but now he lay down again. The boy, too, could not help feeling a tinge of longing inside him.

He said to Arama, 'I know you like the English."

The cacique sighed and said nothing. Ayun looked at the black form in the darkness and his own heart gradually became hard. He said, "I, too, like Dudley but it is only because of the English tongue he taught me. And even Dudley did not teach me all the English I know. Remember the many moons I spent with the English pirates who captured me? They are the ones now that I remember. All the marks on my body, all the whippings. They are the ones I remember. The sea-people are ruthless — *all* of them!" He again mimicked Don Ricardo, growling in Spanish: "You see this sword? This will speak for Spain." Then he said, "Aged One, I hate all the sea-people. Because all they want is gold and they think they own this land and they want to drive us from it. This land is ours and was always here, yet the Spaniard says: 'Colón *discovered* it for Spain.' It is as if Colón had made it, instead of meeting it here. And they all talk of the great cacique, even — even Robert Dudley." A lump came into his throat, despite his bitterness, but he conquered it and hate rose in him again. But in his mind there was the distant voice of Dudley saying, "Elizabeth, great queen, she will be the cacique of all the world. She is in love with Walter, my kinsman." Ayun let his hate and anger drown out this gentle voice, and his face was suddenly twisted with bitterness. He spat. Turning to Arama he said, "Aged One, we must destroy them, these people from the sunrise. I hate them for they mean no good to us. Whenever they come it is to seek El Dorado. All they want is gold, and they want to rule over us."

The old man sighed, "But here there is no gold."

"And that is a good thing. If there was gold perhaps even Dudley would have put us to the sword and driven us out."

"Not Dudley," the old man said, pained.

"No, not Dudley, because he is only one. And so now he would have been lying quietly under the ground. Not Dudley alone, but he had his men."

Arama was shocked to hear the boy. Ayun continued, "They all want this land; I know it. Every night I dream of flocks of white hawks from the sunrise. They swoop down to devour us, and I awake in panic." The old man looked up. The boy went to a corner of the hut and felt for where the poisoned arrows were stacked. Then he said, "Aged One, there will be no cause for fear. I will see that they destroy each other until none is left to trouble us. This land is ours."

There was silence in the hut. Arama's heart was pounding too, because of what the boy had said. Not many moons ago he had dreamt of hawks too. White hawks from the sunrise. And soon afterwards he had got word of the battle in the north, and of Don Antonio de Berrio forcing his way up the Caroni, and of the cacique, Maycay, surrendering land to them, and of the clothed ones from the sunrise building a place of huts and calling it San José. He had been told of the terrifying beasts that the clothed ones had brought with them — frightful beasts, called horses. The northern warriors had broken and run. Hawks from the sunrise! He wondered if the boy's dream had meaning. He wondered what would happen to Curiapan, this Place of the Huts, if—

"Aged One," Ayun interrupted. Arama shook his thoughts away and looked up in the blackness. Ayun said, "The night is thick now. I will go out to the English."

"But you said it is not Dudley!"

"Dudley will not come back."

"But who is it you will see? Is it—?" He was trying to think of Dudley's friend.

But even as he said this there was silence in the hut. Ayun had gone.

1 What are Ayun and Arama talking about?
2 Does Arama want to fight the "sea-people"? Why?
3 Who is Dudley?
4 What do you think is Ayun's plan?
5 Try to find out what actually happened.

10 Mr Wheeler

The story of how Anansi acquired his limp

One day Puss set out on a journey. She loved to travel, often spending days away from home, exploring in the woods and through the savannah country. During her travels she lived by hunting, for she was expert in finding her food, her sharp eyes marking quickly a lizard hiding on the woman's-tongue tree, disguising himself by taking on the white-grey of the tree-trunk or the dull brown of the leaves that hung like tongues from the branches. In all her travels Puss was careful not to cross a river or set out to sea. She was afraid of water.

In the course of her journey, Puss came to a river. She considered what to do. She wanted to get to the other side, but could find no way of doing so. For two days and a night she searched along the bank of the river, looking in vain for a ford. Tired, she climbed a tree that hung over the water and rested, looking at the river.

Who should come by but Mr Anansi, with fishing-rod and a bag for the fish. He fished for half an hour, caught nothing, sat under the tree, wiped his forehead, and said,

"This fishing is a bad business. I have to work too hard. Time to rest now."

Looking around him, Anansi saw the dead stump of a tree. Something sticky was trickling out of a hole in the stump. Anansi touched and tasted the thick syrupy substance near the hole. It was honey.

"What a lucky man I am," said Anansi. "I have found a honey-hole." Trying to get as much honey as possible, he thrust his hand into the hole. Something held him. He could not get his hand free. Frightened, he called out,

"Who holds me? Who holds me?"

From within the stump a voice came, saying,

"Mr Wheeler."

"Wheel let me see," said Anansi.

The hand that was holding Anansi lifted him off the ground, wheeled him around seven times, and threw him fifty yards.

Fortunately for Anansi, he dropped on a large heap of dead leaves and tree moss. The fall stunned him so that he lay unconscious for a five-minute interval. If it had not been for the bed of leaves he would have been killed. When he came to himself he rose, shook himself, felt his hands and feet to see that no bones were broken, stretched himself, then said,

"Out of that little accident I see how to make a living for myself and my family."

Anansi moved away the leaves and moss. He put in their place a heap of stones and broken, sharp-pointed sticks. Then he went back to the tree-stump. Puss quietly watched all that was happening.

Sitting down near the stump, Anansi waited. After a little while, half an hour at the most, Peafowl came in sight. Anansi called out,

"I am glad to see you, Sister Peafowl. A living is here for me and you."

"What is it, Mr Anansi?"

"Come and I will show you," replied Anansi. Rising, he took Peafowl over to the dead stump, showing her the hole and the honey, letting her taste how sweet it was, then said, "Take as much as you wish, Peafowl. Push your right hand inside and take a lot."

Peafowl pushed her hand into the hole. She called out,

"Anansi, something is holding me. I can't get my hand free."

"Pull your hand away," said Anansi. "I will help you."

Anansi took hold of Peafowl and they both pulled.

"Anansi, I can't get my hand away," cried Peafowl, now very frightened.

"Very well then," replied Anansi. "Ask 'Who holds me?' "

Peafowl did so, and a voice answered, "Mr Wheeler."

"Peafowl, tell him 'Wheel let me see'."

The hand wheeled Peafowl around seven times, then threw her so that she fell on the pile of broken rocks and sharp sticks. Anansi ran along with his bag, put Peafowl's body into it, and returned to his place near the stump. Before he could settle himself down, Mr Rat came strolling by, dressed very smartly. He was on his way to see Miss Mouse.

Anansi called out to him,

"I like to see a man dressed up like you are, Mr Yat. I am glad to see you." (Instead of "Rat" he said "Yat".)

'I just bought this suit," replied Mr Rat, "but it cost me a lot."

"Well, I can show you an easy way to get money," said Anansi.

"I wish you would," said Rat. "If I had enough money to live on, I would marry Miss Mouse right away."

Anansi took Rat over to the stump, showed him the honey, and said,

"Put your hand into the hole. You will find the sweetest, thickest honey there."

Rat pushed his hand in. Mr Wheeler held him.

"Anansi, Anansi!" cried Rat, who was a very nervous man. "Help me, man, help. Something is holding me."

"Ask who holds you."

"Wh-wh-who is holding me?" stammered Rat, who was so terrified he could hardly utter the words.

The voice from within the stump said, "Mr Wheeler."

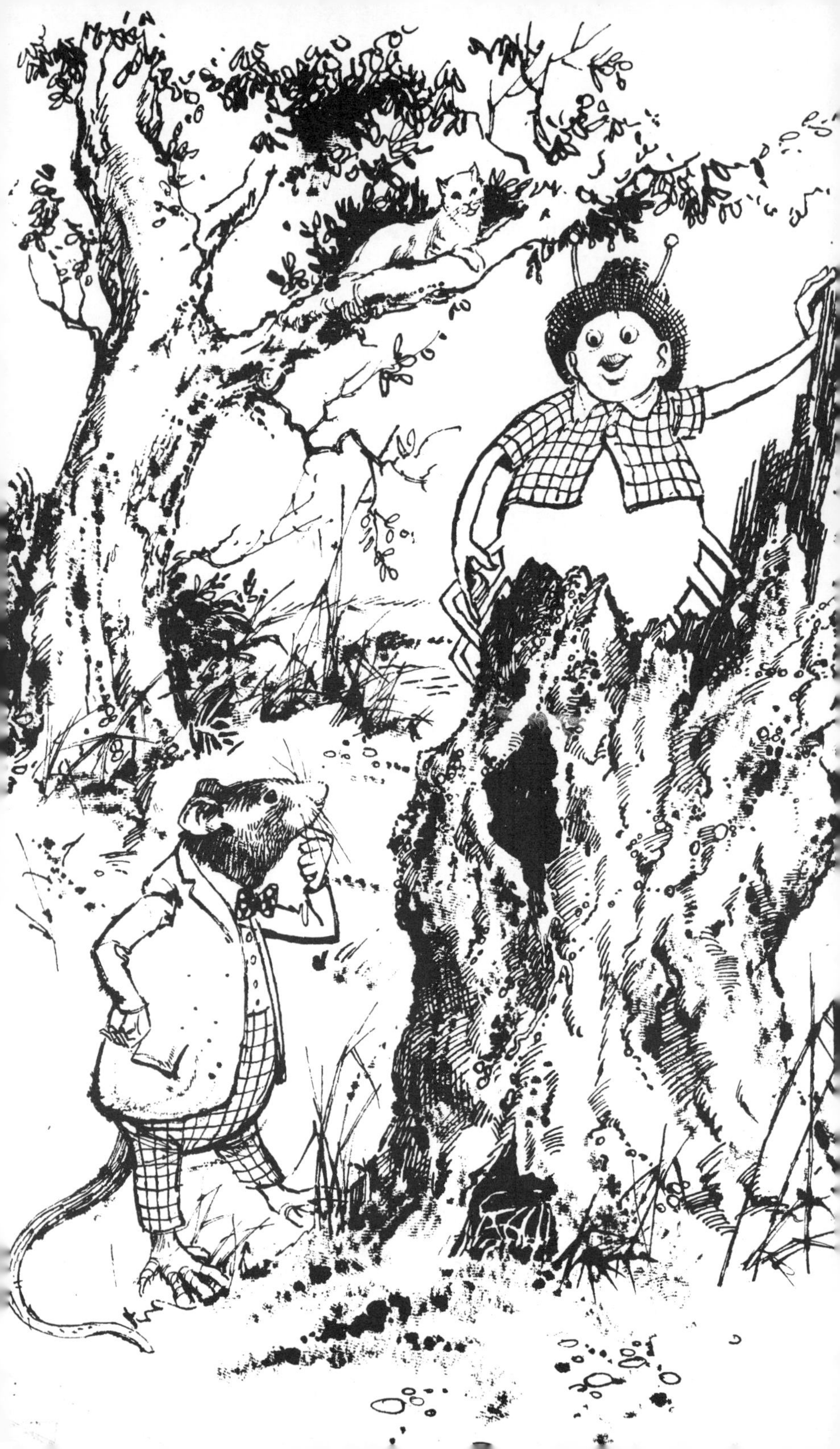

"Oh, Mr Yat," said Anansi. "This is easy. Tell him 'Wheel let me see'."

Mr Wheeler wheeled Rat around seven times and threw him. Anansi ran along, picked up Rat's body, put it in the bag, and returned. While Anansi was gone, Puss climbed down from the tree.

After Anansi had returned to his place near the stump, Puss came walking by. Anansi was very glad to see her, for Puss was plump and likely to be very tasty. He called out,

"Good morning, Puss. I am very glad to see you."

"And why are you so glad to see me, Anansi?" asked Puss.

"Walk over here, my good friend Puss, my dear sister, and I will show you why I am so glad to see you. Come and see how we can both make a living."

Puss went over to the dead stump with Anansi.

"Look at all that honey, Puss. Taste it."

Puss pretended that she could not see the honey. She said, "Honey, Mr Anansi? I don't see any honey. Give me some to taste."

Anansi touched the honey on the outside of the stump with his finger and gave it to Puss to taste. Puss said, "Yes, this is very good honey, Anansi, very good honey. What a pity there isn't more of it. Now that you show me I can see it glistening on the tree-stump. What a pity there is so little of it. If there were a lot we could make a good living."

"But there is a lot, Puss!" said Anansi angrily. "There is a lot in the hole. Just put your hand in."

"Anansi, I don't see a hole. Is it here?" Puss pushed her hand away from the stump.

"You must be blind, Puss," shouted Anansi, who was fast losing his patience. "My mother told me you were stupid, but I never believed her until now. Here is the hole, here."

Puss pushed her hand in the other direction.

"Here, Puss, here. Watch my hand." Losing his temper completely, and eager to catch Puss, Anansi accidentally thrust his hand into the hole.

Wheeler held Anansi's hand.

Anansi began to cry. Tears fell from his eyes. Thinking of the jagged stones and the sharp-pointed sticks, he cried out, "Puss, something is holding me."

Puss said, "Ask who holds you."

Anansi replied, "I know who is holding me, Puss. Look, my friend, you know how I love you. I will give you everything in that bag if you will do what I ask you."

"What is that?" asked Puss.

"Run along very quickly, Puss, along the bank of the river for fifty yards, to a place where there is a heap of rocks and sharp sticks. Move them away, dear Sister Puss, move them all away. Spread in their place as many soft leaves as you can find, just as if you were making a bed."

"But, Anansi," replied Puss, "what a funny thing to ask. You are in trouble; you are my friend. I can't leave you alone.'

"I know what I am asking you to do," said Anansi. "And you must do it quickly. Pull some of the long, dead banana leaves from the trees and spread them out. Put some moss also. Make the place soft, soft."

"Well, said Puss, "I really don't like leaving you here, but I will do what you ask."

Puss ran along, and removed the rocks and sticks, though not all of them for she meant to teach Anansi a lesson. She spread the leaves and moss, but did not quite cover the remaining stones. Then she hurried back. She found Anansi in a state of desperation, with beads of perspiration on his forehead. While she was yet a long way off, he called out, "Did you do it?"

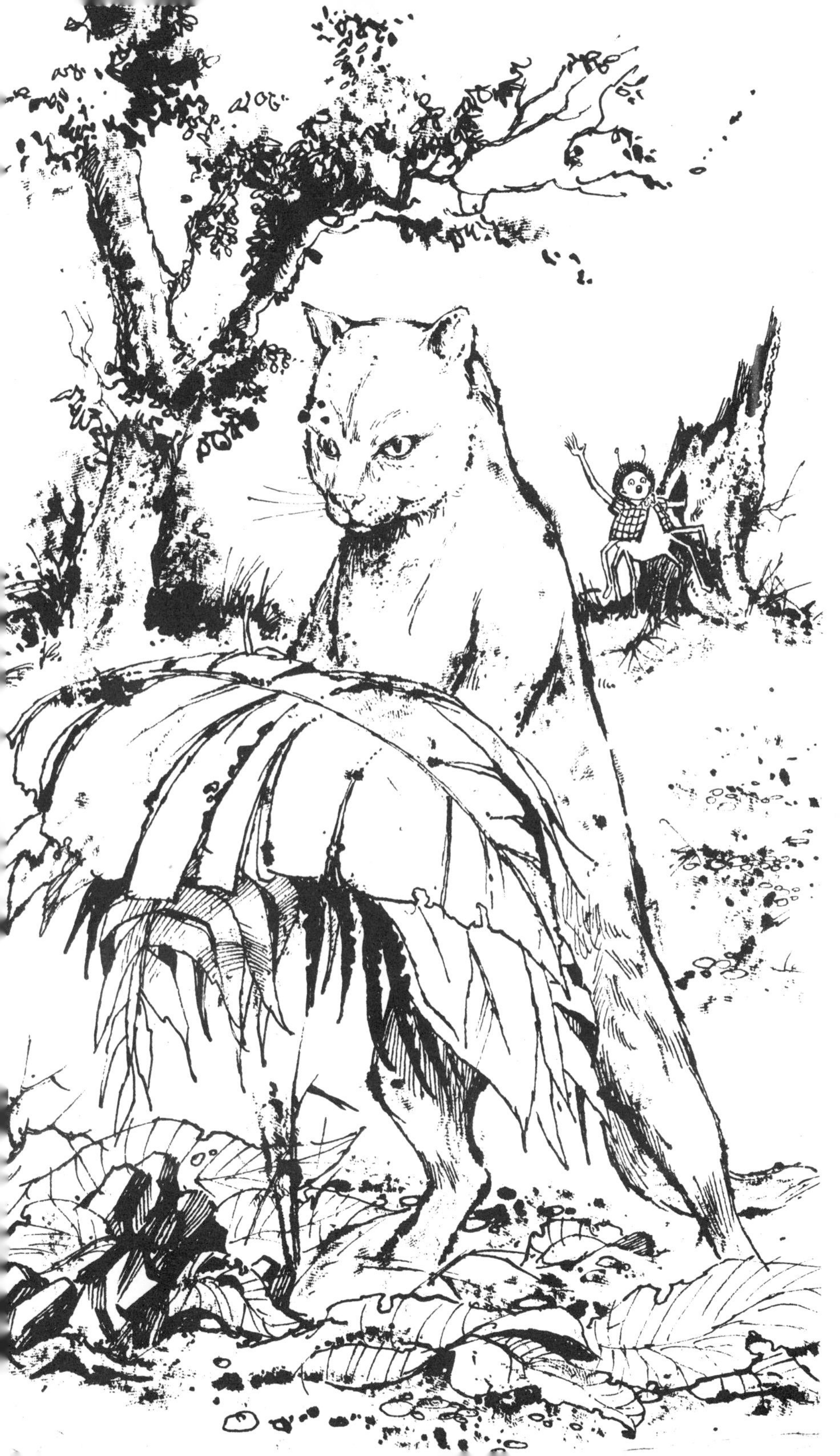

"Everything is ready, Anansi."

"How do you mean that everything is ready?" asked Anansi anxiously. "Did you spread a lot of banana leaves, Puss?"

"Everything is ready, I think, Brother Anansi."

"Look, Puss, you had better run back just to make sure. Run and bring me one of the banana leaves, so I will know you have done what I asked."

Puss went away for ten minutes, and returned without the banana leaf. She said, "Anansi, you must believe me. Everything is ready."

Anansi felt the grip on his hand tightening. He knew he had no more time. Trembling, he asked, "Who holds me?"

"Mr Wheeler."

"Whe-wheel-l-l-let me see."

The hand wheeled Anansi round seven times and threw him. He fell on to the bed of leaves, but he hurt his leg on the rocks that Puss had left beneath the leaves. Puss picked up the bag with Peafowl and Rat in it and went on her way home.

As for Anansi, to this day he walks with a limp.

from WEST INDIAN FOLK-TALES
by PHILIP SHERLOCK

1 How did Anansi intend to 'make a living'?
2 Why didn't Anansi see Puss at first?
3 Imagine that you are Puss. Write a letter to your cousin, Tiger Cat, telling him about the incident.
4 Find the name of the lizard that changes its colour to suit the surroundings.
5 Say whether the following statements are *true* or *false*.
  (a) Peafowl lost her life because she trusted Anansi.
  (b) Puss was looking for a bridge in order to cross the river.
  (c) Anansi was smart but Puss was smarter.
  (d) Puss's action saved Anansi's life.

11 Noise

I like Noise.
The whoop of a boy, the thud of a hoof,
The rattle of rain on a galvanised roof,
The hubbub of traffic, the roar of a train,
The throb of machinery numbing the brain,
The switching of wires in an overhead tram,
The rush of the wind, a door on the slam,
The boom of the thunder, the crash of the waves,
The din of a river that races and raves,
The crack of a rifle, the clank of a pail,
The strident tattoo of a swift-slapping sail—
From any old sound that the silence destroys
Arises a gamut of soul-stirring joys.
I like noise.

JESSIE POPE

12 North and South

O sweet are tropic lands for waking dreams
    There time and life move lazily along.
There by the banks of blue and silver streams
    Grass-sheltered crickets chirp incessant song;
Gay-coloured lizards loll all through the day,
    Their tongues out-stretched for careless little flies.

And swarthy children in the fields at play,
    Look upward, laughing at the smiling skies.
A breath of idleness is in the air
    That casts a subtle spell upon all things,
And love and mating-time are everywhere,
    And wonder to life's commonplace clings.

The fluttering humming-bird darts through the trees,
    And dips his long beak in the big bell-like flowers.
The leisured buzzard floats upon the breeze,
    Riding a crescent cloud for endless hours.
The sea beats softly on the emerald strands—
    O sweet for quiet dreams are tropic lands.

                                CLAUDE MCKAY

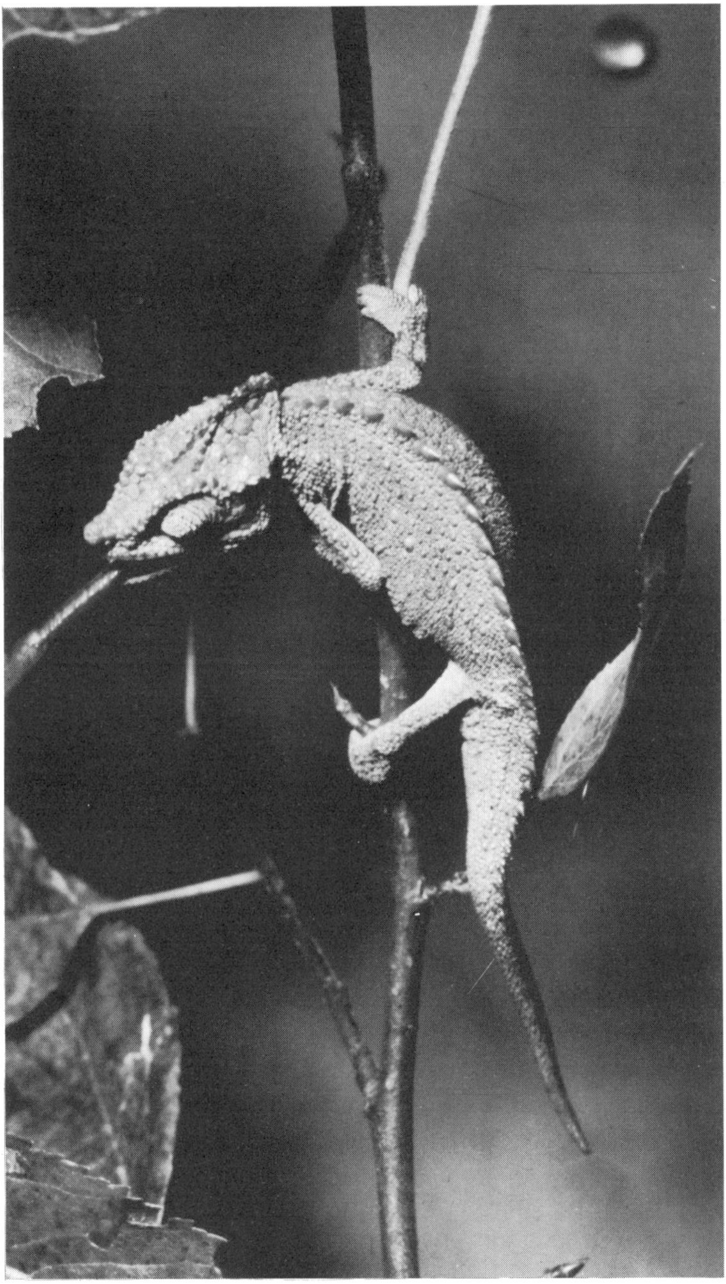

13 Examinations

As the days went by, Sprat could not help becoming more and more frightened of the examination. As the pressure mounted with revision tests, extra lessons, extra homework and the great rush to borrow books that no one had bothered with a month before, Sprat began to wish that it was all over. At night he dreamt of arithmetic tables marching up and down in columns. He saw forests of litmus paper turning blue, yellow, green, red—all sorts of colours. In one dream Junjo was locked up in a glass jar, and they were all to pour something into the jar. When Sprat's turn came, Junjo suddenly changed into a shark and jumped up at him from the jar. Mrs Morrison bought him a bottle of bitter tonic, which he hated. Aunty sent him one of her specials, compounded of honey, rum, pimento and various secret ingredients. It tasted delicious and his father had half the bottle.

Mother Rebecca came up with the best help, as might be expected. It was Saturday, and Sprat was disconsolately multiplying 46·75 by 1·38. He did not like decimals. The point kept going into the wrong places, and every time he worked the sum he got a different answer. Mother Rebecca, when appealed to, said that she was no genius, and had left school more than fifty years before anyway.

"Don't you have friends who can do that stuff?" She looked over his shoulders at the messy exercise book, where blots jostled with crossed-out work, and a few holes showed where Sprat had erased something a little too energetically. "I don't mean someone like your Dad. He'll just do it for you, and you'll never find out *how* it's done. You need some child in your class to show you how."

Sprat thought for a moment. One of his problems was that he did not like to ask questions in class, and so he often got left behind. Junjo was even worse. He hated to admit that he did not know everything, and he was scared of looking foolish in front of the whole class.

"What about that little girl I met last week?" asked Mother Rebecca. "Let her come down here, and bring a few others—not more than two or three, mind you. Between the pack of you, you should be able to figure out enough and more than enough to please any inspector, Shark or no Shark."

So that evening Blossom was launched on a career that led after many years to a post as lecturer in mathematics at a large technical college in Kingston. No one would have guessed it, watching her on the floor of Mother Rebecca's little room, her shoes kicked off in a corner, and the ribbon missing from her spiky plaits. Sprat's mother had given them several sheets of yellow and blue cartridge paper, and Blossom set her 'pupils' to work all together on one sheet of paper. They did easy sums and hard sums, and Mother Rebecca looked up the answers in the back of Blossom's arithmetic book. They kept at every sum until even Junjo (who had begged to be in the class) knew why it worked that way.

On Sunday after church they were back at it, drawing maps of the West Indies and the main geographical regions of the world. Junjo had not the faintest memory of some of these things.

"Tropic of Cancer," he said, writing this along the Equator. They were now filling in a blank map of the world.

"That's wrong," said Sprat. "That's the Equator."

"No, it's not," insisted Junjo. "The tropics are in the middle, so it must be the Tropic of Cancer. Jamaica is in

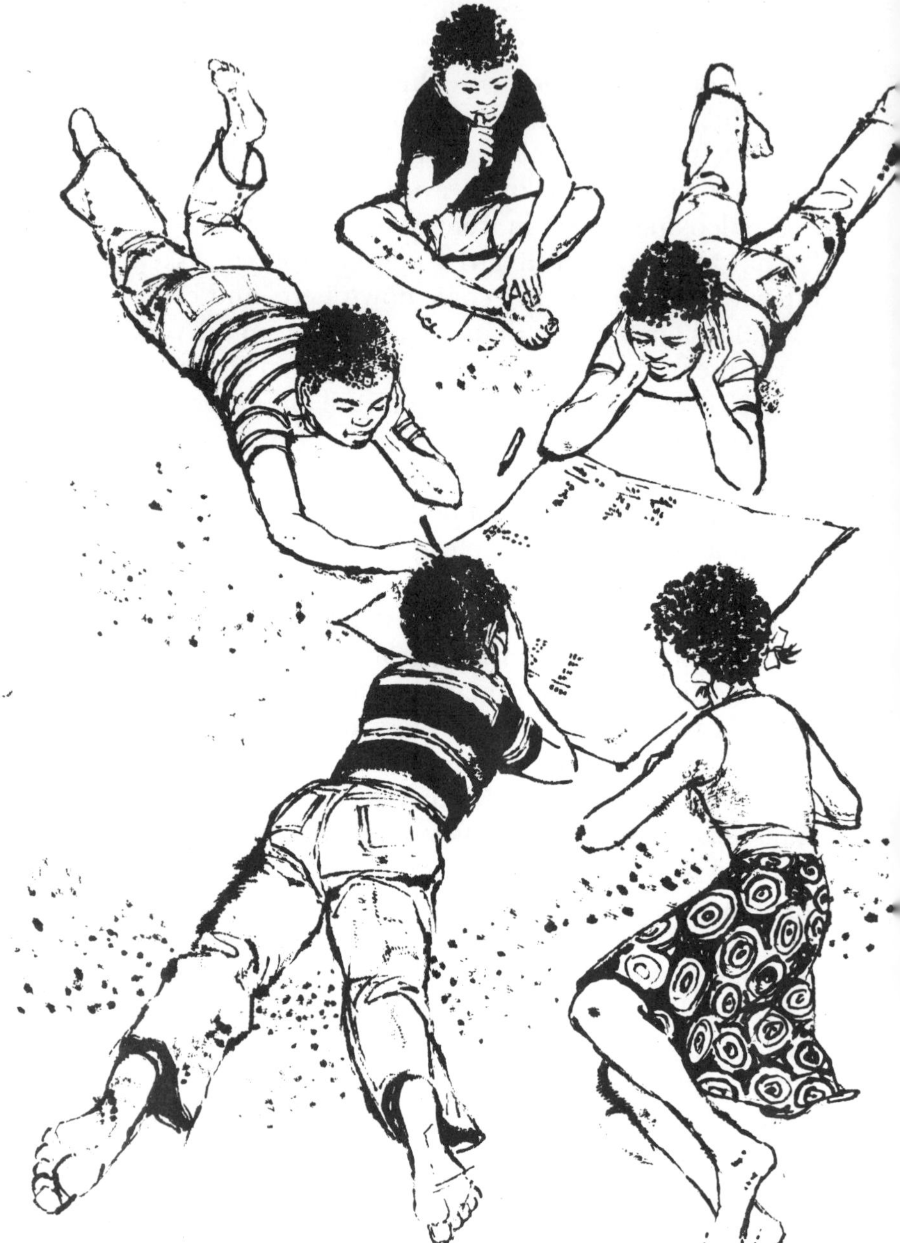

the tropics," he added condescendingly.

"Then what about the Tropic of Capricorn?" Sprat asked. "You can't put the two of them in the same place!"

"I don't know about any Tropic of Capricorn," grumbled Junjo. "You must have made that up."

They were not supposed to look at the atlas until they were finished, so Sprat had to defend himself by argument alone.

"Look here, Junjo," he said more patiently. "We always have three lines across the map, don't we?"

"Those are the Arctic Circle and the other one, and the Equator. That makes three." Junjo was stubborn.

"Well, five in all, then. I mean we have one in the middle, and two half way from there, and then the North pole and the South pole. Right?"

"Mmm. H'mm. All right." Junjo was not sure of his ground.

"Well, the one in the middle is the Equator, and the other two half way ones must be the Tropic of Cancer and the Tropic of Capricorn."

Something stirred in Junjo's memory, and he nodded. After much argument they agreed on which was in the north, and which in the south. Then they went on to Junjo's favourite subject: the deserts of the world. Only the good Lord knows why he was so intrigued by this aspect of geography, when he found the rest so easy to forget. What is more, he could spell all the names of all the deserts correctly, and this for one who could not write a letter to his grandmother without two spelling mistakes at least in every line. He also could show you on the map where each desert occurred, but he had no idea of the names of the countries where they were found. Sprat knew all this, and was grateful when Junjo allowed him to write the word 'Sahara' across the middle of North Africa. Then Junjo took over.

The crayon scraped along the stiff paper.

"Down here," he muttered, "A-t-a-c-a-m-a Desert. Over here Kalahari. Up here Arizona. In here Gobi. Oh yes. Sinai desert. And Tundra up here. Mmm. Yes. One more." He marked the Central Australian Desert.

Blossom looked over his shoulder.

"But you people haven't even put in the names of the continents!" she cried. "Junjo, you shouldn't have put in the deserts so soon!"

Before long the map was a mass of green, brown and red crayon, and Sprat had to draw the main rivers in black.

Blossom giggled.

"Those rivers must be full of dirty water," she said.

Junjo and Sprat were now arguing about the mountain ranges. Junjo said there were none in Africa at all. He put in Mount Everest (forgetting the rest of the Himalayas), and said that he was hungry, he was going to drop down if he didn't have something to eat.

To tell the truth, they had been working for more than an hour and a half, and that is long for spending on the same thing. Mother Rebecca was surprised they had stuck to their work so long, and meanwhile she had prepared a suitable reward.

"This will keep your strength up until you get home for lunch," she said, bringing out four large mugs of lemonade and a plate of bun and cheese. The bun was a very special kind, dark, moist, and spicy, and it came all the way from a bakery in Montego Bay. They ate all of it. May put her head through the doorway and was given a slice by Sprat. She took it to her corner in the shade of the ackee tree, and seemed to enjoy it as much as anyone else.

Later in the week the friends met twice again, and went over some history and health science. Sprat continued to dream about maps where real mountains and rivers appeared, and strange flowers and plants grew on the pages of his exercise book, but he had no more nightmares. They meant to have a last meeting for sums and tables, but in the end there was no time.

On the morning of the first examination everyone was early for school. The children stood around in the yard and out in the road before first bell, fidgeting and snapping at each other. Junjo alone appeared calm. He explained to Sprat that he had failed so many examinations that this was nothing. His mother had given him a long lecture that morning on 'Facing Up to Life'. She had also given him a brand-new pencil case with a neat little sharpener fitted into one end. The set contained a pair of compasses (very handy for jabbing your neighbour in the arm or leg), a set square and a protractor, the use of which were quite beyond Junjo. Still, they were new and very impressive, and Sprat was quite envious when he saw how everything fitted into the folding plastic case. Alvin was also in a boasting mood, having been promised a real fountain pen if he did well. Nobody asked how well he would have to do in order to qualify for the reward.

Soon the bell rang, and they assembled for prayers and roll-call. Miss Watkins chose a prayer from her book. It was her favourite, and bits and pieces of it lingered ever after in the memories of all her pupils. Even Junjo, working years later as a customs officer with children of his own, sometimes recalled snatches of the prayer. Few of the children understood it when they first heard it, for the sentences were long, and none of them were much inclined to think about things like prayers and sermons. They usually found them bewildering and boring. But years of standing in the schoolyard for prayers, with the morning sun streaming between the trees and the silence broken only by Miss Watkins' voice, stored in the mind of every child the words and feeling of the prayer.

'Help us, O God,' read Miss Watkins, 'to stand for the hard right against the easy wrong. Save us from habits that harm. Teach us to work as hard and play as fair in thy sight alone as if all the world saw. Forgive us when we are unkind, and help us to forgive those who are unkind to us. Keep us ready to help others at some cost to ourselves; send us chances to do a little good every day . . ."

Her voice echoed across the open yard, and for once even the boys in the back rows were still. Sprat wondered why right was hard and wrong was easy. Then he remembered his decimals, which were still giving trouble, and sighed.

Soon they were all filing inside to the places where they would sit for the examinations. The smallest children went off to the open-air classrooms on the far side of the playgrounds. They were not having real examinations, but would spend the day doing tests in reading and writing, and they would make picture books and posters with cut-outs from old magazines. It seemed very unfair to Sprat and his friends. They were in Fifth Grade, and were put to sit in between rows of Third Grade children. Miss Fisher, the Third Grade teacher, handed out writing paper and rough paper, and the fun began.

On the first day they had geography and arithmetic. On the afternoon of the same day, they had the English composition paper. Junjo said at lunchtime that he thought he had got everything right in the morning, but the afternoon brought disaster. In the composition test, they had four subjects to choose from:

    A ghost story,
    My plans for the summer holiday,
    A letter to a friend describing my visit to the zoo,
    My best friend.

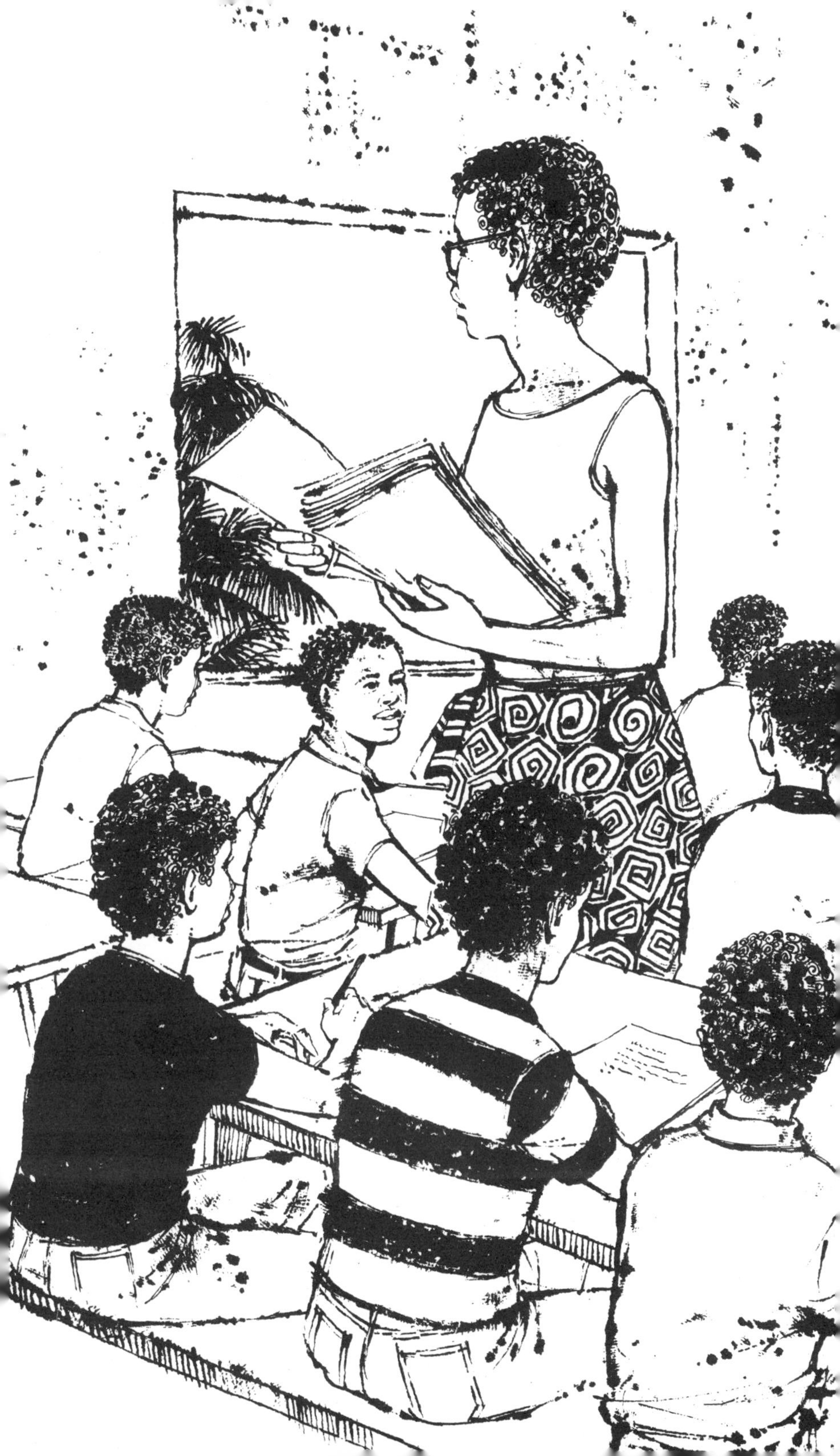

Poor Junjo decided to write about his best friend. He started writing about Alvin, and then couldn't find anything to say after the first sentence, which ran, "My best friend is the rudist boy I kno."

Somehow that did not seem quite the right opening, so he crossed it out and spoilt the page. He then chose Sprat, and tried again, "My best friend is the fatist boy in schul. He eat a lot of different things. One day his pants berst when he bend down. They had to sow it up for him to go home and it berst agen on the rode. He is a good fellow thogh."

At this point Junjo's mind went blank. Nearby he could see Cynthia Williams writing page after blotty page. She even asked for more paper and got it. In the row across Alvin was writing slowly but surely. He finished a page and a half, and drew a neat double line. Blossom Wright, just behind Cynthia, had finished long before and handed in her composition. Those who finished early were allowed to read a book in the remaining time, and Blossom was looking at a large book from the Junior Library. It was called *The Story of Our World*, and contained incredible pictures in lurid colour of monsters, storms, volcanoes, sunsets, birds and lizards. A picture of some ancestor of the iguana caught Junjo's eye. He wrote on.

"My best frend look like a historic monster."

He chewed his pen.

"He ave a big belly and feet like sticks. I guess if he fell in the gully they culd dig him out and put him in the mesiam."

After much thought he added the conclusion.

"Enyway I like him and he helpt me with gegraphy and hischry for exams. He is qite good at lessons and sometimes share lunch with me."

Sprat wrote a ghost story about a haunted bridge which no one could cross after midnight on a Friday night. His mother had told him the story several times, for it was his favourite. He was so absorbed in writing that he hardly noticed how time passed. In what seemed no time at all, Miss Fisher was telling everyone to stop writing and hand in their papers. He just managed to scribble his name on the second sheet of paper before she came to his desk and took it from him.

Three days later, all of the examinations were over and still the Inspector had not come. Sprat and his friends began to wonder if it had all been a mistake. In a few days the term would end, and beyond that stretched the glorious vacuum of the summer holiday. Once more there was talk of camps in the mountains, of trips to the sea, and of Alvin's grandmother down in farthest Hanover. Mrs Morrison replied to all of Sprat's inquiries that she "did not know. Go and ask your father." Mr Morrison was hardly any more helpful, and told his impatient son that when the holidays came, they would see. Sprat was left feeling that everyone else was doing something exciting, and he would be all alone until his friends came back for the September term.

from SPRAT MORRISON
by JEAN DA COSTA

1 Why did the children fidget and snap at one another on the morning of the first examination?
2 We knew what two of the children became when they grew up. Which two children are they, and what did they become?
3 Correct the errors in Junjo's composition. Some are spelling errors and some are grammatical mistakes.
4 'Those are the Arctic circle and the other one and the Equator'. What is 'the other one'?

14   The Quarrel

I quarrelled with my brother
I don't know what about,
One thing led to another
And somehow we fell out.
The start of it was slight,
The end of it was strong;
He said he was right,
I knew he was wrong.

We hated one another.
The afternoon turned black.
Then suddenly my brother
Thumped me on the back
And said, "Oh, *come* along!
We can't go on all night—
I was in the wrong."
So he was in the right.

            ELEANOR FARJEON

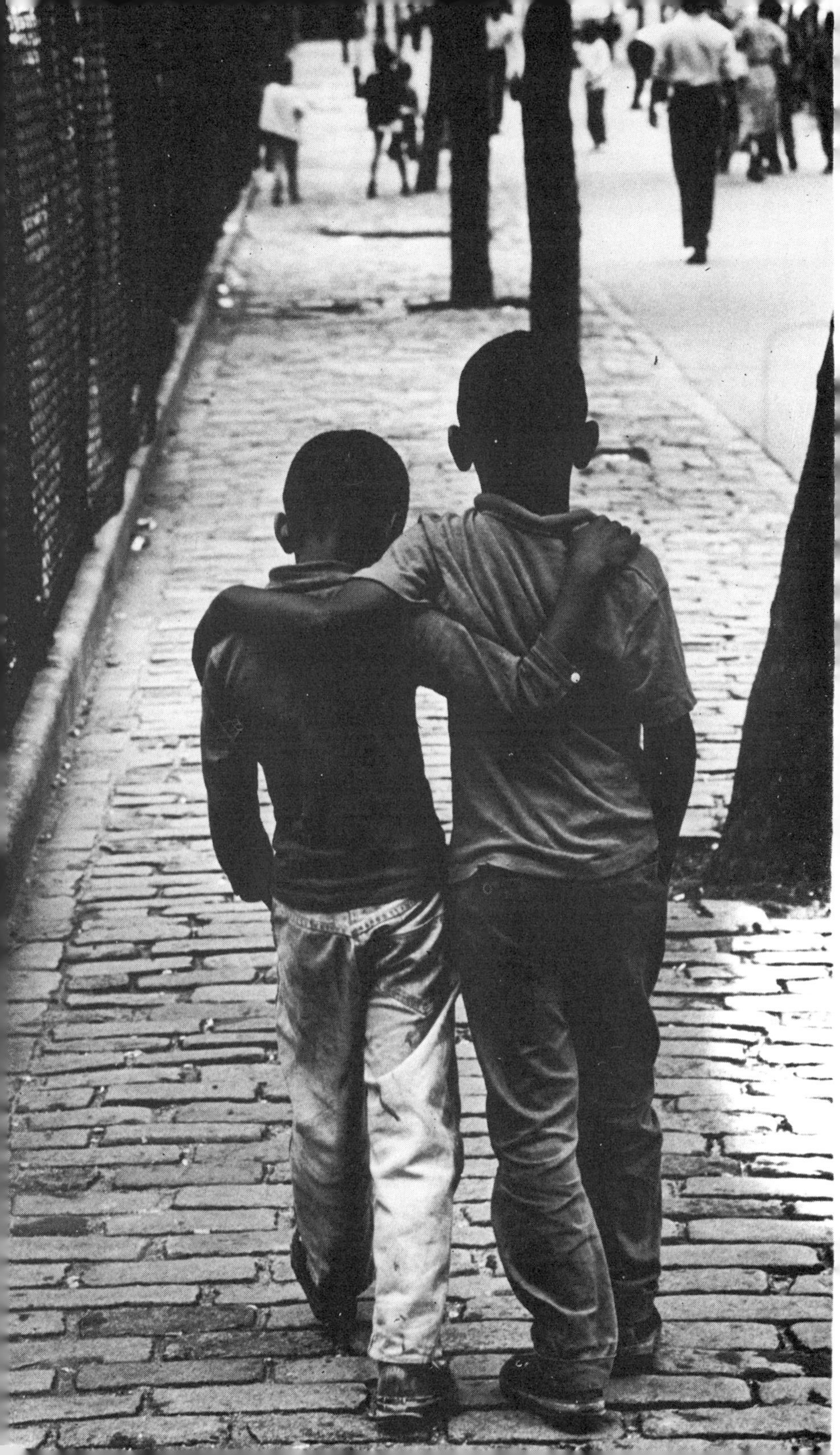

15 The Master Sisserou of Dominica

The first people to live on the island of Dominica were the Arawak Indians. Once there was an Arawak Indian Chief called Sisserou who lived in a cave on a hillside. A group of hunters secretly followed the Indian Chief one day, and his path led them to the cave on the hill where he lived. After arguing among themselves, they decided to venture into the cave. They found him covered with the coloured feathers of a parrot! The hunters were impressed by the deep green and violet feathers, and they thought he must have divine powers. So they started to worship him by praying to him and asking him to tell the future. Soon they began to ask him favours. In order to grant their wishes he gave them the things they had asked for from his cave.

One day a woman came to him and asked him to give her a child. Knowing he did not have a child in his cave, he became afraid that others would find out he did not have supernatural powers. Late that night he crept out of his cave and set out to sea. Some say that the steps from his cave that led into the sea can still be seen between the Carib lands of Wakaresi and Kraibu.

From out of the clouds a large, full-bodied green bird flew over the quiet blue of the Caribbean Sea. Early morning mists were slowly rising from the waters.

The greenish-blue head of the bird turned towards rugged volcanic peaks shrouded in clouds. The precipices were covered with green patches. As he flew closer to earth his red eyes could see that the land was covered with palm trees, breadnut trees, mango trees and many other trees of the rainforest.

The wings of the bird beat rapidly as he flew to a nest high in the branches of a breadnut tree. He was very excited to be coming back from the heavens above the clouds.

This was the Master Sisserou! It was his duty to fly to the heavens and bring messages back to Dominica. He was the guardian of Dominica and the soul of the Arawak chief.

On this day the Master Sisserou had an urgent message. He landed in his nest in the hollow of the great branches of the breadnut tree. From the dark cavern in the tree top his voice echoed:

> *Seastorm waters are near*
> *Whistling winds bring fear*
> *Landslips will take the earth*
> *Heed what our trees are worth!*

His voice vibrated out from the hollow in the breadnut tree into the valley and across the mountains. Even the wild animals understood the Master Sisserou. All the people of the valley, the mountains, the villages and the towns heard him.

Flocks of animals began to gather themselves in preparation. Many birds flew to the neighbouring islands of Martinique and Guadeloupe. The people who lived on the coast watched with growing concern when they saw large parrots flying away from Dominica. Shop owners nailed boards over their windows to keep the winds out.

The Master Sisserou began to search for seeds and fruit in the tall trees of the rainforest. While he hunted through the forest he heard the voices of the noisy Sisserou chicks. He knew that while the chicks were growing they would need more and more food. He had watched their parents feed them once a day, twice a day, three times a day, sometimes even four times a day! Luckily there is usually only one new chick hatched each year in a Sisserou family. It takes a lot of work to get the food the chicks need and a lot of time to teach them what to eat and which animals will eat them—and grown parrots too, if they are hungry enough!

The chicks stay with their parents until they learn where to find the flowers, seeds and fruit in the high branches of the rainforest. The Master Sisserou thought of the many miles they might fly in search of food when they grew up to become adults.

He landed in a small flock of birds drinking water from the giant green orchids which grew in the dead branches of tree crowns. They were chattering noisily about the coming storm and what they could do when it came. The Master Sisserou described how he was filling his nest with food.

A small parrot landed beside him. Shyly he looked up at the Master Sisserou. He stuck his beak bashfully into the water for a quick drink. He felt his feathers grow warmer as he listened to the words of the Master Sisserou.

"Store seeds and fruit in your nests for the young chicks to eat. Together we will find a safe place for our families."

The young parrot believed the Master Sisserou. He would protect them and lead them to safety. Just as the small bird looked up from the water, big drops of rain began to fall.

The sky went from light blue to grey. Ever darkening clouds quickly crossed the island, and the wind started to howl. It became very different for the birds to fly. The winds beat against their wings as the sky turned white with rain.

Palm trees swayed so close to the earth that the green fronds were touching the ground. The large limbs of the breadnut tree began to break. Walls of rain fell on many of the large trees in the forest, and loosened the tree roots from the earth. Strong winds tore up the trees and then came crashing down to the forest floor.

The Master Sisserou wanted to fly far away from the wind and rain. He was thinking about the other parrots and their young ones. How would they survive the storm? Heavy rains could flood the roosts and drown the chicks. They could not fly without the wind bending their wings backwards, perhaps even breaking them. He also knew he could not stay in his nest if the trees began to break.

So he started the long climb down the tree using his beak and feet. When he reached the forest floor he noticed that the wind was not quite as strong. Now the greatest danger was from falling trees and branches.

The Master Sisserou began to search for a hiding place. Other parrot families followed him. They were not used to being on the ground, because they usually explored the high branches of the rainforest. Flood waters began to rise, and the rapid gullies of water were strong enough to sweep a large bird away. Just as the parrots were about to be blinded by gusts of sea water, the Master Sisserou saw a large cavern.

With great difficulty, climbing against the wind, he used his beak to dig into the crevices of the cliff. Finally, he reached the entrance of the cavern and led the parrots behind him into its cool darkness.

The wind continued to howl for many hours. Rain blew into the cavern but the parrots remained safe. They huddled together, chattering softly to reassure their mates and young ones.

It seemed as though a very long time had passed when they heard the wind fall quiet and the howling outside begin to fade away.

"Waak-waak!" the parrots squawked as they edged out of the cavern. "Waak-waak!" It was over! To celebrate the end of the storm they rolled over on their backs, stretching their legs whilst the rain fell on their throats and bellies.

Fluttering his wings, the Master Sisserou soared into the sky. As he flew over the once green earth, he looked down and saw that the mountains were now brown and barren. Landslides toppled the trees down the slopes like brown sticks.

Tall royal palms were snapped in half. In the villages, galvanised roof-tops were strewn over the remains of broken furniture. Only a few large trees were left. The breadnuts, the mangoes and the coconuts lay on the forest

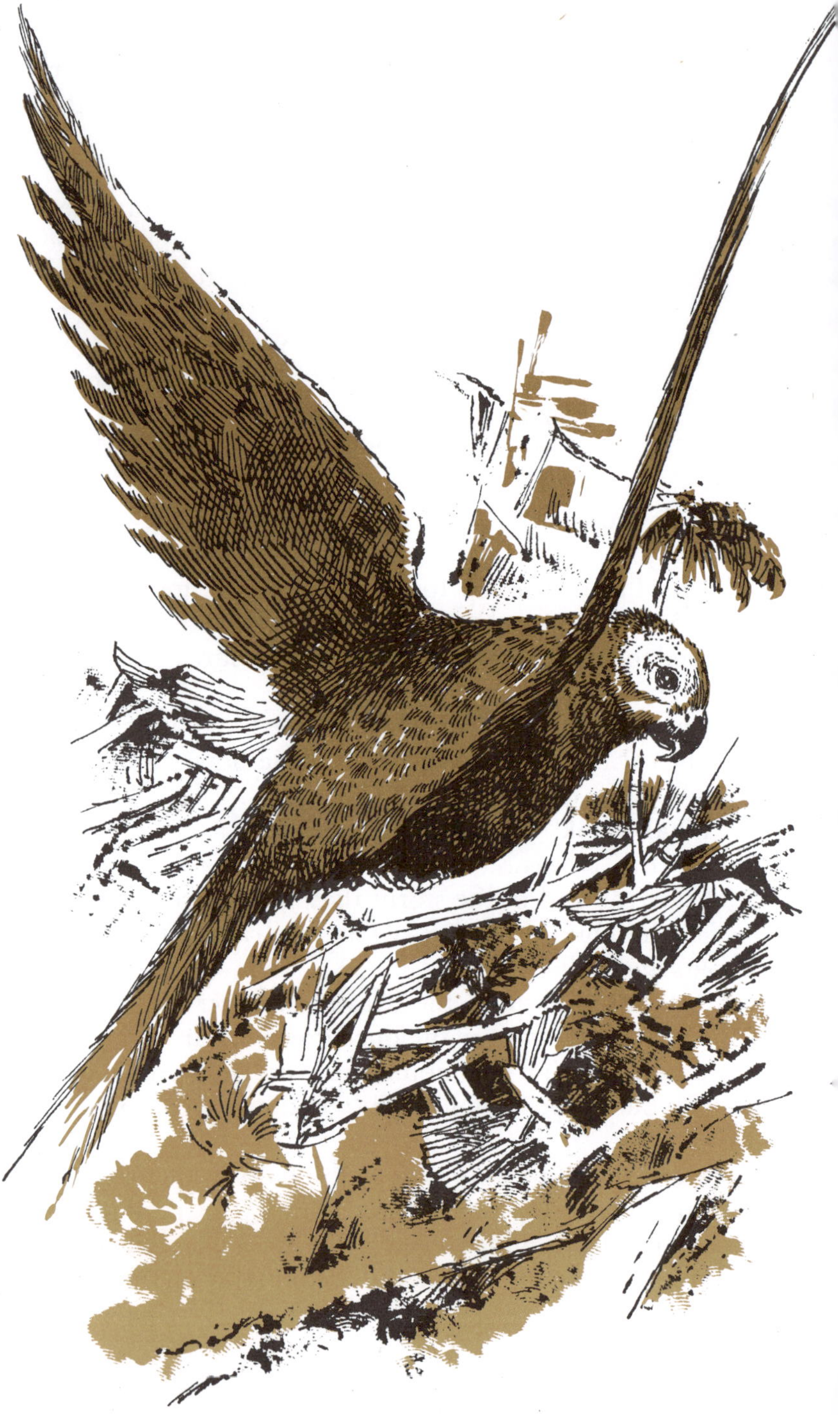

floor. A few people clambered out of the piles of boards that used to be buildings.

The Master Sisserou wanted to close his eyes. He could not bear to see any more. Just as he was ready to turn back to the cavern, he saw that brilliant bands of pink, yellow, blue and purple now encircled the island! A rainbow as magnificent as the sun shone across the sky.

The Master Sisserou was filled with hope. It was time to return to the heavens and bring a message back for the people of Dominica.

Many parrots were swept away by the wind. Many were injured. Only forty survived after the hurricane. As they left the cavern they were eager to rebuild their nests. They began to search for food and breadnut trees in which they could build a home for their families. For many hours they flew over the island but there were few trees left that had large enough branches for nesting. Some parrots landed in the villages of Calibishie and Bells, hungry and exhausted. The children of the villages shared the coconuts and mangoes that had fallen during the storm with them. The parrots were so hungry that they also ate bits of boiled rice and bananas that had been left on the ground.

The sound of hammers hitting metal rose up from the villages. People were putting up blue tents that the helicopters had brought from faraway countries, because their homes were filled with water and some were even blown apart.

Lumberjacks came to the island. They cut and sawed and cut and sawed. Trees that had fallen during the storm were transformed into smooth planks and slabs ready for builders to use.

The parrots cried, "Creek-creek! Creek-creek!" as their old tree homes were cut into pieces. When the fallen trees were sawn into pieces and stacked up, the people of Dominica suddenly realised how beautiful the rainforest had been. They wanted to see the earth green and alive with plants and fruits. They wanted to see the birds flying above the trees, bringing seeds from distant lands into the soil of Dominica.

However, the lumberjacks were filling their pockets with the money they made from wood. They gazed upon the few trees left after the storm. In these trees they saw more wealth for themselves. They were not ready to leave.

Businessmen were already scheming to sell to each other the land the people had learned to treasure. The restless parrots screeched to each other. The agouti and the iguana scurried into the bush. The crapauds jumped along the streams and croaked loudly to the land crabs.

The animals of the rainforest were anxious and frightened. If the lumberjacks cut down the rest of the trees they wondered what would happen to them.

"Dominica, an island without trees?" they asked each other. What would it be like?

The people in the villages were talking too. "We need to find work," they told each other. "There are many jobs with the lumber companies."

"But," said some, "after the trees are cut and the buildings made, what would be left of the island for our children?" Just brown and barren earth, they thought to themselves. A shiver of fear ran through the village.

The parrots looked into the heavens each day for the return of the Master Sisserou. But they did not see him.

And then one bright moonlit night a strange mist began to creep up from the floor of the rainforest. The animal calls were silenced as the tree spirits or zombies appeared. They roamed the forest mountains in search of their homes—the figuier and fromager trees which the lumberjacks had chopped down. While the zombies wandered in the rainforest they found the piles of sawdust left by the lumberjacks. The large saws and drills and axes of the lumberjacks became immersed in a heavy mist. The lights of the houses where they were staying suddenly went out! Shrill cries pierced the stillness of the night.

Some of the old Carib Indians said to themselves, "We

knew it would happen. We never cut the larger fromager or figuier trees. We never used kapok from these trees for pillows because our grandfathers had warned us that if we did we would be haunted."

The next days the lumberjacks found their saws and drills and axes where they had left them, but when they tried to cut wood the tools would not cut. Their tools were as dull as they could be. When they tried to sharpen the tools their files broke in half.

The Caribs warned them, "The zombies are after you. You have cut their tree homes down. Do not eat the fruit of the trees you have cut and do not use the wood for houses or furniture or they will cast a spell on you."

But the lumberjacks did not listen. They ordered more tools for cutting and sawing from other countries. They decided to stay on the island and wait for their saws and drills to arrive.

The people of the villages became frightened. They tried to talk the lumberjacks into leaving Dominica.

"Please go, for your own safety. You have finished your work here. We must leave the rest of the trees alone."

"We are not afraid of your spirits!" they scoffed. "If you want Dominica to grow you must have more business. And how can you have more business unless you have more buildings!"

But the people did not believe the lumberjacks were thinking of Dominica. Except for the lumberjacks who lived in wood houses, the people continued to live in tents. They shared the food they had with each other, and helicopters brought canned meats and provisions from far away countries. But everyone wondered what they would do when the canned foods were eaten. Before the great storm there had been plenty of bananas and coconuts and breadfruit but most of these trees had been blown down during the storm. How many years would it take for them to grow back and produce enough to feed the people of Dominica?

Each day the people went to fetch fresh water from

streams close to their tents. Tete-chien began to appear. Children counted one, two, four, eight, slithering over the clay roads. Each day the villagers saw more tete-chien creeping over the boulders and broken asphalt in the road. It was very unusual to see so many out in the open.

"What does this mean?" they asked each other.

It seemed there were more tete-chien around the wooden houses of the lumberjacks.

"What is going to happen?" they cried. "We told the lumberjacks to leave!"

Just when they were sure the worst was about to happen a voice echoed from a high cavern in the rainforest. It was the Master Sisserou! He had returned from the heavens with a message for the people of Dominica.

> *Arise, arise!*
> *Dominicans arise!*
> *Mountains and rainbows reign*
> *Over green earth and sugar cane.*
> *Join hands as the quaking land*
> *Devours the hardened selfish man!*
> *Sisserou will sing free*
> *In the branches of the breadnut tree!*

His voice echoed out from the cavern in the rainforest into the valley and across the mountains. All the people and animals of the valley, the mountains, the villages and the towns heard him.

News from the Master Sisserou warmed the hearts of the people. Everyone came out of their tents and hugged their friends and neighbours. They were there to help each other and face together whatever difficulties were ahead.

Hearing all the commotion outside, the lumberjacks decided to come out of their houses and see what was going on. But when they tried to get up from their chairs or walk across the wooden floors of their houses, they could not move! They were stuck to their chairs! They could not move their feet off the floor. In horror they tried to move their hands and legs but slowly they began to melt into the wood. Their flesh became part of the wood itself. Some say that as they felt their bodies melting, the voices of the tree spirits were chanting: "Whenever anyone looks at a piece of wood, they shall see the faces of the lumberjacks melted into the wood they wanted so badly..."

Outside the people in the villages began to feel a trembling of the earth beneath them. Cups and bottles fell over, and the metal poles holding the tents swayed. The people clung to each other tightly. The earth around the houses where the lumberjacks had been living gave way, and their wooden houses collapsed like houses of cards. The dark earth swallowed them.

The rest of the island was left unharmed.

Later, many people walked to the place where the earth had covered the wooden houses. They found pieces of wood and noticed how the grain in the wood looked like tiny eyes, noses and mouths.

Even today if you look closely at some pieces of wood you can see the sad faces of the woodcutters melted into the wood by the zombies.

The Master Sisseriou flew over the earth that had closed over the houses of the lumberjacks. They would never disturb the people of Dominica again. The land had been given to the people of Dominica because they realised the importance of the trees and the unspoiled beauty of the rainforests that cover the mountains. In time, the trees left on the barren hillsides would become green once more. There would be homes in the high branches of the breadnut trees for frail Sisserou chicks. They would bathe in the rain showers and grow up to pair with other Sisserous for the rest of their days on the island of Dominica.

RIA MERCADO

1 Who was the Master Sisserou?
2 What did he look like?
3 What was his role?
4 What news did he bring to the animals and birds of Dominica?
5 How did he save the Sisserou parrots from the storm?
6 Describe the land after the hurricane.
7 How did the people live after the huricane?
8 Why were the zombies angry with the lumberjacks?
9 What lesson does this story try to teach?

16 Theophilus Albert Marryshow

For a very long time many of the islands of the West Indian archipelago were ruled by Britain. As a result, the people of these islands spoke a common language, though most of them came from Africa, India, and many other parts of the world. They enjoyed the same climate, the same trees and flowers, the same vegetables and fruits. They all grew sugar cane and depended on this main crop for their economic prosperity.

With so many things in common it was natural for them to be united in other ways. Soldiers from all the islands enlisted to form the Caribbean and West Indian regiments; athletes banded together to represent the West Indies in international competitions, and cricketers from many islands played together in the West Indian Test team. Finally, higher education for all the islanders centred in the University of the West Indies.

This co-operation was natural, but many people felt it was not close enough. They wanted the islands to federate, and so come together as one large, strong nation.

One of the most enthusiastic supporters of federation was Theophilus Albert Marryshow. He devoted his life to this cause, so that he eventually became known as the Father of the Federation. He lived to see his dream come true when the Federation of the West Indies was formed in 1958, and he died in the same year. Thus he was spared the pain of seeing the break-up of the association four years later.

Theophilus Albert Marryshow was born in 1885 in St George's, the capital of Grenada. His family were devout Wesleyans, and as a small boy he attended the Wesleyan primary school. His parents were very poor and he was not able to go to school beyond the primary stage.

He spent his early boyhood in the Montserrat area of St George's. In a district known as the 'Tanteen', a happy playground for all children, he and his friends set traps for doves, caught crabs, and stole plums and sugar apples. He was a typically high-spirited boy. He knew every inch of the Tanteen and every boy and girl who lived there. He was popular with them all.

When he left school he was apprenticed to a printer. Later, he became a reporter, and it was now that he met a man who greatly influenced his life. This man was William Galway Donovan, a fearless journalist and editor of the *Federalist* and *Grenada People*. Donovan was a tireless supporter of West Indian federation, and he spoke and wrote on the subject with equal fluency. He passed on his enthusiasm to the young Marryshow.

At this time Marryshow was an active member of the Grenada Literary and Debating Club, and it was here that he developed his talent to communicate. He became a first-class debater, and soon made a reputation both as a speaker and a writer. As he matured, he became an even more ardent advocate of West Indian unity. He found many willing listeners, for he was a young man of considerable charm and pleasing appearance.

So it was that in 1913 Marryshow founded a newspaper which he called *The West Indian*. In his paper he condemned social injustices of all kinds, and when he felt that criticism was justified he did not fear to attack the administration or even the Governor himself. But his main concern in the newspaper was to press home his arguments in favour of federation.

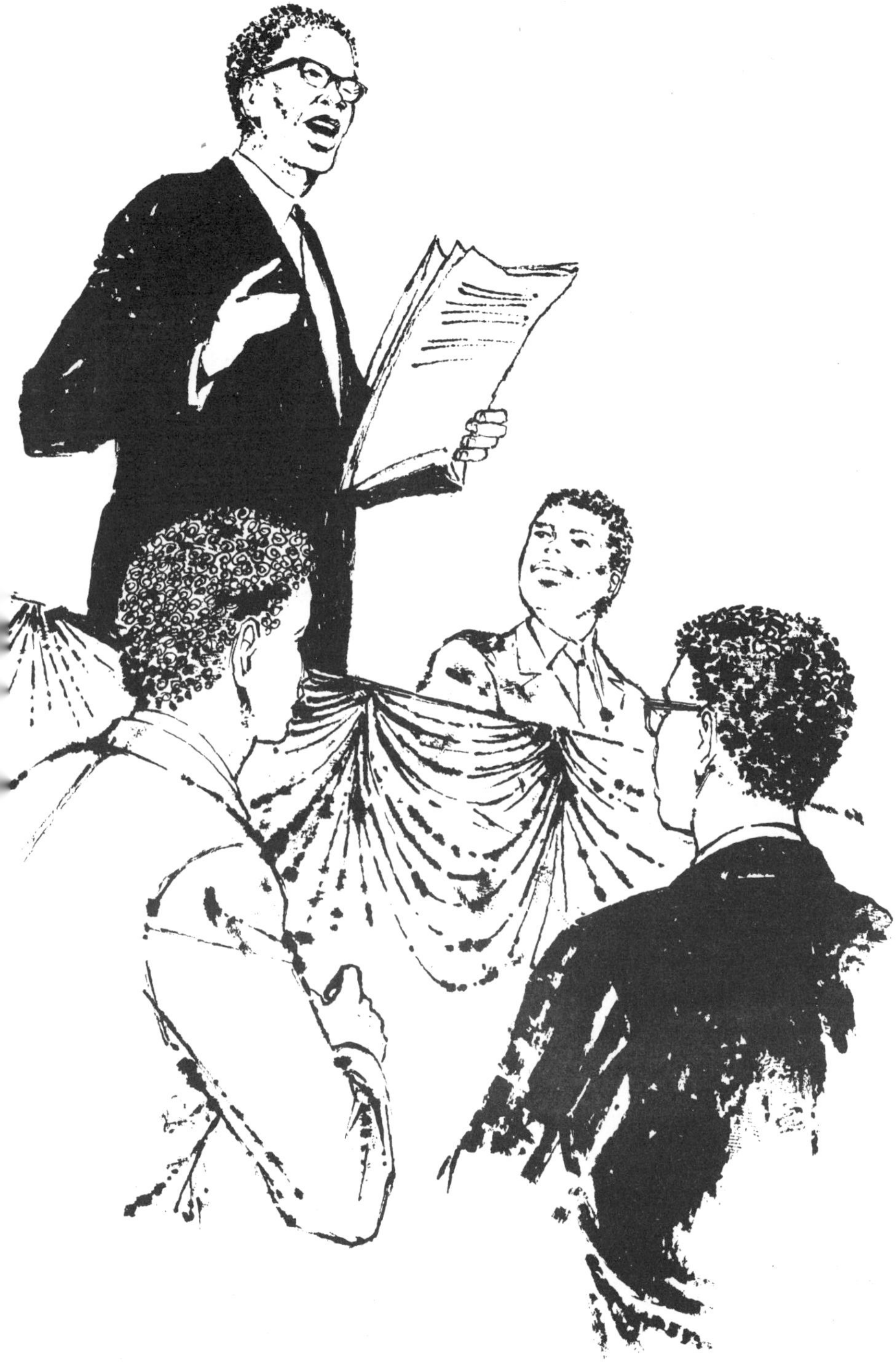

In one article he wrote: "A West Indies in a world like this must unite or perish. This is not the time for parish pump policies. We must think nobly, nationally, with special regard for the first fundamentals of a West Indian unity, and a West Indian identity."

He began to travel around the islands of the West Indies where he met and talked with other leaders about federation. His tall figure, always elegantly dressed in a vicuña suit, and his polka dot tie, became a familiar sight in political circles. His charm and eloquence always assured him of a welcome.

In 1925, when Grenada gained representative government, he entered politics in the general election in Grenada. He won a seat representing St George's, which he held for the next thirty-three years, an all-time record.

When the West Indies Federation was formed in 1958 he was nominated for a seat in the Senate, but almost immediately he was taken gravely ill. From Port-of-Spain he returned home to Grenada, where he died on the 19th October, 1958. A long and distinguished career had come to an end, and leaders from all over the Caribbean attended his funeral. It was fitting that they should pay tribute to a great representative of the West Indian people.

from GREAT WEST INDIANS
by THÉRÈSE MILLS

1. Find out the names of the territories that were part of the West Indian Federation. How many of these countries are now independent?
2. Who was chosen as the Prime Minister of the Federation of the West Indies? Who was the Governor General?
3. Why was Marryshow called the 'Father of the Federation'?
4. Find out what you can about CARICOM.
5. What is an 'archipelago'?

17 The Master Kite

It suddenly occurred to me that I was hearing some sort of sound and then I realised that it was the radio playing. Radio music was a very unusual thing in this house. It was playing very softly, very low. I wondered, was Mr Chandles back. I did not hear him come in. If he was back he must have walked in very quietly. It was even stranger to think of him walking quietly. I felt a sort of inner amusement. Not the sort of amusement to make me laugh aloud. I got up from the patch of sun and went down into the yard. I could not see anyone in the schoolyard, but I had just heard voices over there. The blueness of sky around the coconut tree was a bigger blueness now. Presently I heard the voices again and two boys came running around the other side of the school. They were trying to put a kite up. This made me interested right away. Of course it was December. The kite season already! Well, January was the kite season. Still . . .

The boys ran up and down along the flat place beside the school. The bigger boy was in front holding the reel of thread and the small one was trying to give a lag. But the kite would not go up at all. I laughed. Every now and again the big boy came and examined the kite and he was in a bad temper with the smaller boy because the kite wouldn't go up. But the reason was not the smaller boy. Anybody could see that the tail wasn't long enough. If you had a Mad Bull kite you had to give it plenty of tail. The thread, I could see, was all right, but they had to put on plenty more tail. They could even put two long strips. They stood on the pavement side, the smaller boy standing on the pavement itself to give

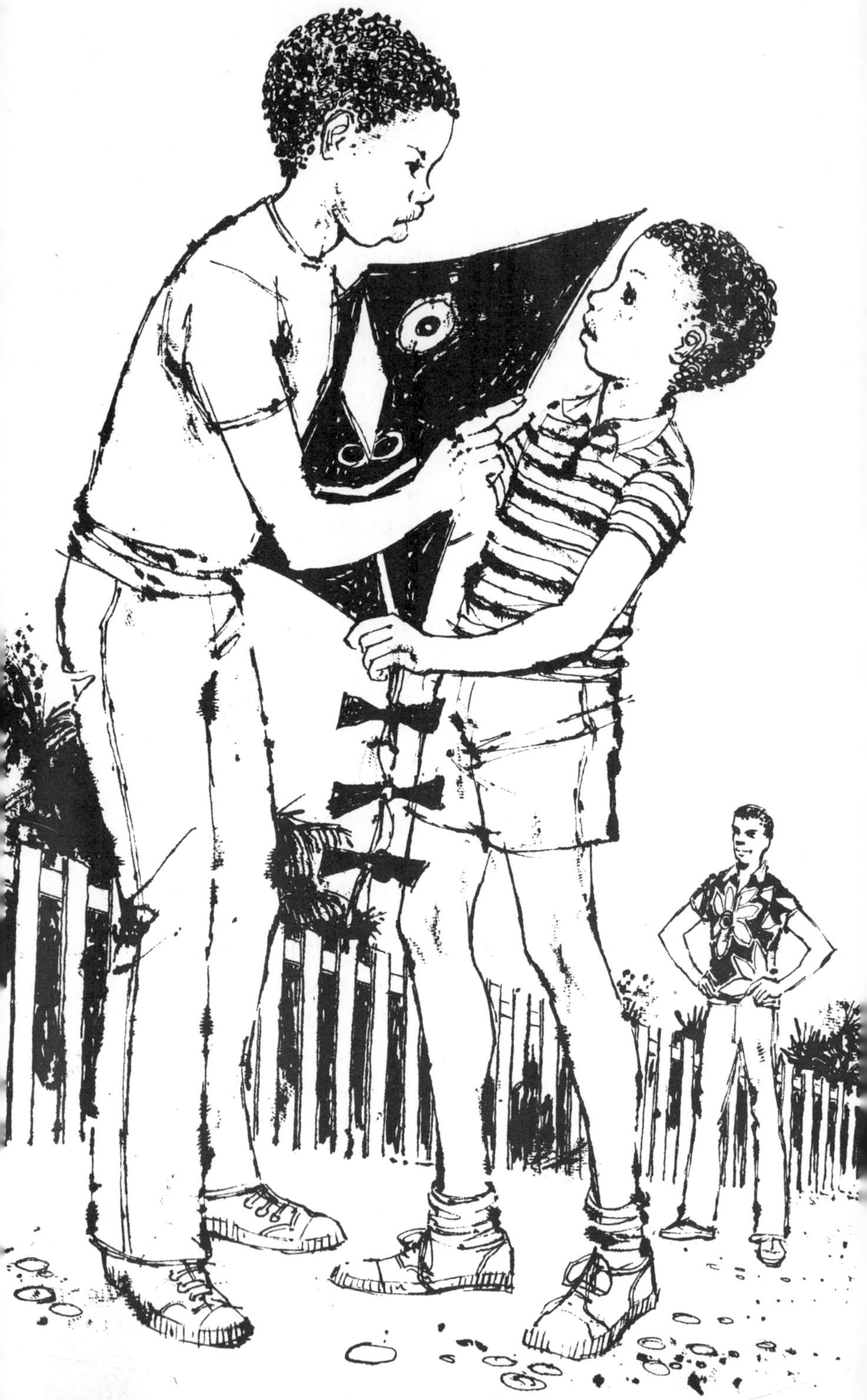

more height, and they both were at the ready and then the bigger boy cried "Now!" and the smaller one let go and the other came running backwards into the wind. I didn't want to shout out to him because now the place had to be very quiet, with Mrs Chandles sick, and in any case Mr Chandles might be inside. I made a sign to attract him—the bigger boy—and when he watched I made him a sign to say the tail was far too short. I then pulled my right hand vigorously along my outstretched left arm up to the shoulder, showing that the tail had to be at least so long. But they could not understand. I put my hands beside my mouth and I said, "Tail!" "What?" they shouted. I made them the sign meaning, Come over here.

I took the kite in my hand. It was such a strong well-made kite, it was a pity they did not know about it. The ribs were big and strong. They were made of strip bamboo. Those were the sort of ribs for a Mad Bull kite. This had the right quality paper too and real Mad Bull colours. It was a pity these fellers couldn't appreciate it. If you had a Mad Bull you had to know how to fly it. It didn't take any fool to fly a Mad Bull. I held the kite out before me, picturing it up there playing with the clouds. When it was up there you had to know how to hold it. You couldn't give too much twine at first unless the wind was in your favour. These little fellers were really too light to fly a Mad Bull properly. I could imagine the Mad Bull wanting to go and them trying to hold it back. I wanted to laugh. Anyway this was a first-class kite. The feller who made this knew about making kites.

"Who make this kite?" I said.

"Uncle," the smaller one said. I supposed the bigger one wanted to say *he* made it.

"You have a master kite," I said.

I couldn't think of any rags indoors that I could tear

a tail from. There was a piece of my bedding, though, that should make a good tail. I didn't want to go inside to do that if Mr Chandles was in.

    I couldn't help laughing at the ridiculous little piece of tail they had tied on. It was a miracle how the kite hadn't nose-dived on the yard and got broken up. I turned to the bigger boy. He was only a little smaller than me but he had no kite-sense. "Listen," I said, "you want plenty more tail here. For this to go up you want tail all this . . ." I had stretched out both my arms to show him the length. "All that," I said.

    If you hadn't very heavy tail, that was the length to put. When Felix made Mad Bulls that was what he put. You could tie on a zwill, too, if you wanted. A razor blade would be a good zwill for this one. If you had a new razor blade, and you were a good kite-man it wouldn't take a minute to cut any twine cleanly and send the other kite flying across the village. I wondered if anybody would cut this kite down. I had the sneaking feeling that this kite wouldn't last. I could picture a good kite-man fixing on a sharp zwill then sending up his kite to have a few words with this one. I couldn't talk for laughing. "You putting a zwill?" I said. "What?" the bigger one said. "Okay," I said, "okay, don't worry!" They were laughing heartily too though they couldn't tell what I was laughing about. "Go and get a good strong tail," I said. "Ask your uncle."

    I kept them just a minute longer while I loosened the compass, pulled it down a little and drew it tight, then I gave the kite back to them. They ran out and across the street, excited. I didn't know all that much about kites but I was a professor compared to those two. They knew absolutely nothing. They were out of view now. I looked at Celesta Street a little. Evening was closing in and yet I was feeling the heat of the sun on my head. I went up into the passage to listen to see if Mrs Chandles was still groaning. Then I came back to have a look at the ducks.

from A YEAR IN SAN FERNANDO
by MICHAEL ANTHONY

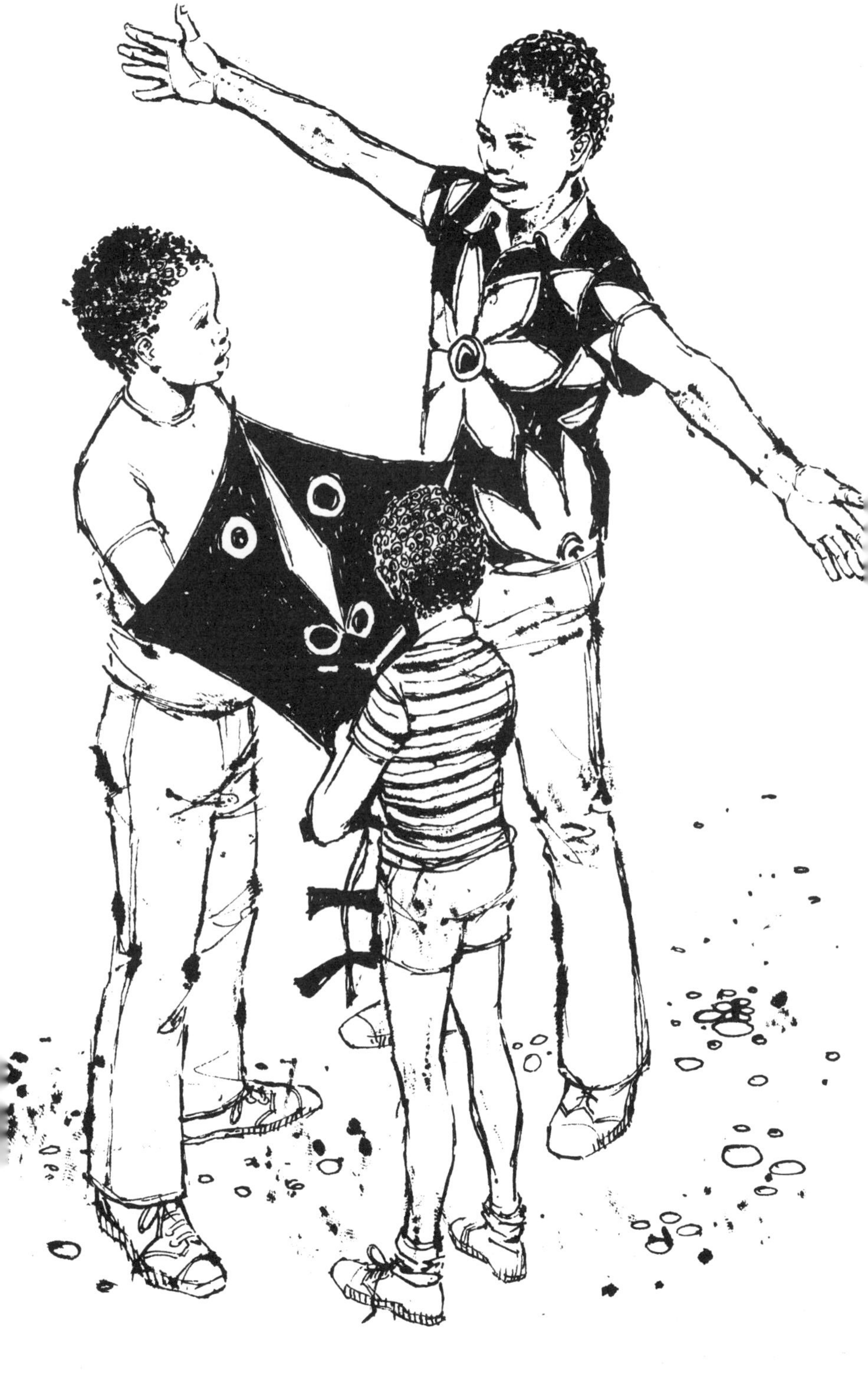

1 Apart from a long tail, what are the 'characteristics' of a good Mad Bull kite?
2 Why do you think the bigger of the two boys would have liked to say that he made the kite?
3 Who knew the most about kites, the narrator, the two boys, or Felix? How can you tell?
4 What would be needed to defend the Mad Bull kite in the air?
5 "Okay, don't worry!" Why did the narrator let the matter drop at that point?

18 The Incas of Peru

The sun shines brightly in the Cusco Valley this morning. Our Sun Gods are happy and we are happy because they are pleased with us. Today is a special day. Today marks the beginning of the ploughing season. The Great Fair is held on the first day of the ploughing season.

Today the villages all over the land will come together to trade their goods and to celebrate. This Great Fair is going to take place in the Holy Square. The Holy Square surrounds the Temple of the Sun, our largest and most important Temple.

Today perhaps my father will let me get a baby llama. I can learn to ride my baby llama as he grows older. When I am a 'puric', in other words a full grown man, like my father is, I can use my llama to help me carry my goods. I will not kill my llama for meat as my people do, even though the llama meat is delicious. I will keep my llama forever.

Suddenly I hear my name being called. "Pacha!" "Pacha!" At first I think it is my father calling me to work. No! It is my friends. They are my Inca brothers. They call me Pacha. But it is not my real name. My real name is Pachacutec, which means 'All-teacher'. It is the name of our Great Emperor, Pachacutec. I was called after him because he is a great and wise man. All my people love him. He is the son of the Great Viracocha.

My father says that Viracocha was greater than his son Pachacutec. He says that Viracocha made our Empire as big as it is today. They say our Empire is very big but I cannot imagine how big. Cusco Valley is so big and it is only a small part of our Great Empire. My father, who knows many things, says that our Empire stretches over the mountains, down onto the coast of the Great Ocean on the West. When I grow older I will become a soldier and fight for my Emperor, our Sapa Inca. I will march over the mountains and go down onto the other side to see this Great Ocean. My father says that one day our people will learn to build ships and conquer this Great Ocean, and our Empire will be even greater.

Again I hear my friends calling, "Pacha! Pacha!" I know they want me to come out and play. Today we will play soldiers. We will play on the Great Bridge which was built long before I was born. My father says it was built long before he was born. I do not believe him. It does not look so old. It is sturdy and the strong cables of aloe that hold it to the huge pillars look new.

Even those massive pillars look new. My friends and I have tried to climb these pillars. My father says this is very dangerous, for if we fall we shall surely die. This I believe, for we can hardly see the bottom of this deep gorge over which the bridge is built.

We will play soldiers, crossing the bridge on their way to conquer more tribes. We will play soldiers, if my father lets me go out and play. He told me that today was not a day for play.

"Today is a day for work, Pacha. We have to get our goods ready for the Fair. You are the oldest, Pacha, you must help your mother and me."

Yesterday I helped my father for the whole day. We dug up the potatoes we cultivated and packed them in bags. We hope to trade our potatoes at the Fair. We need more meat and we have no more llamas to kill. My father is extremely proud of these potatoes. He once told me that potatoes first grown by my people were as small as pea grains. Now he grows potatoes as big as the balls we used for play. I think my father should write a book, for he tells such fantastic stories.

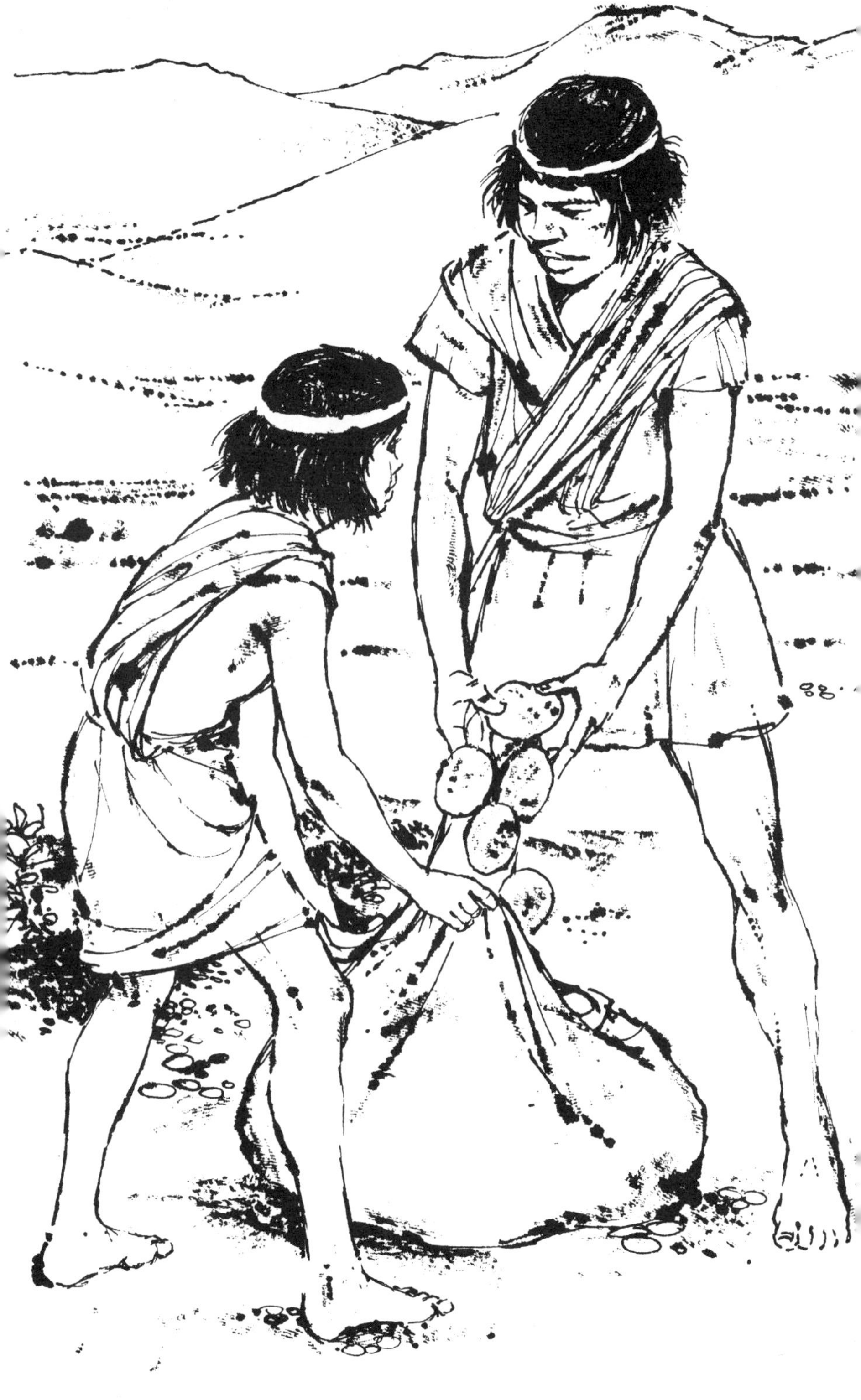

Yesterday I also helped my mother pack her best weaving. She hopes to trade this fine cloth for some pots for her kitchen. She will surely get many pots for her beautiful weaving. She will not trade her best cloth today but will keep it to give to our Sapa Inca Pachacutec as a gift. She believes that our Sapa Inca deserves the best, for he is the best puric in the Land. He has always been kind and generous to all the villages. He has been especially kind to our people here in the Cusco Valley. Perhaps it is because our Inca Empire began in this valley a long time ago, and he has a special love for those of the Cusco Valley.

Let me tell you more about our Emperor. He is called Sapa Inca, which means Sole Ruler. He has given to our people good roads, strong bridges and sturdy comfortable houses. All families have enough food to eat. No one goes hungry or goes without the things he needs. Sapa Inca punishes the officials if any family suffers. He has appointed officials, each of whom takes care of ten families, and the officials are all kind and compassionate. Here in Cusco Valley we have all that we need. Our Sapa Inca has built long irrigation canals to bring water to all the villages and so our land gets enough water to be fertile and to produce fine crops. Last year when my baby sister was born, Sapa Inca gave my father an extra plot of land to cultivate to get more food to feed the extra mouth.

Sapa Inca is a very learned man. I think he is more learned than his best priests, for he often asks them questions that they cannot answer.

Sapa Inca once said, "The noble and generous man is known by the patience he shows in adversity."

He is a noble and generous man, for he shows great patience with the people who do wrong things. He merely has them flogged if they commit offences that are not serious. If someones does commit a serious offence, he is hanged. Not many people of my village commit serious offences. The main reason is that they are contented and do not get into mischief. They have no time for idling. When they have finished working their fields they go into their houses to eat and chat, or play with their children. My father usually spends his free time doing his featherwork. He is a very skilled feather worker. He is not so skilled a builder of roads and he prefers to spend his extra time doing this kind of work. He will give his best pieces of work as a tribute to our Sapa Inca.

He will give this gift to our Sapa Inca today. I think it may be better for me to stay and help my father. Perhaps he will let me go with him to present our gift to the Sapa Inca. What a privilege it will be to see and talk with the Great Emperor Pachacutec.

I will help my father. As I look around I see the villagers busying themselves with their packing. It is time to start moving the llamas into the roads. Some strong fathers carry heavy loads and have started walking behind their llamas. On their backs they carry jugs of *chicha* to give to the Sapa Inca and for themselves. I have never drunk *chicha*. My father says it is a very strong beer. Only the purics in my village drink *chicha*. Some even get drunk if they drink too much. I think there will be much *chicha* drinking today at the Fair. Maybe I can get a taste when my father is not looking.

I see more and more people on the roads. All are heading for the Holy Square. I must hurry. My father is also on the road with his bags. He is looking for me to help him.

Now we too are on our way to the Holy Square. This square is a very large place. Thousands and thousands of people gather here. The Holy Square of Cusco Valley was built many years ago, yet the stones are still in fine condition. My ancestors dragged these huge stones for

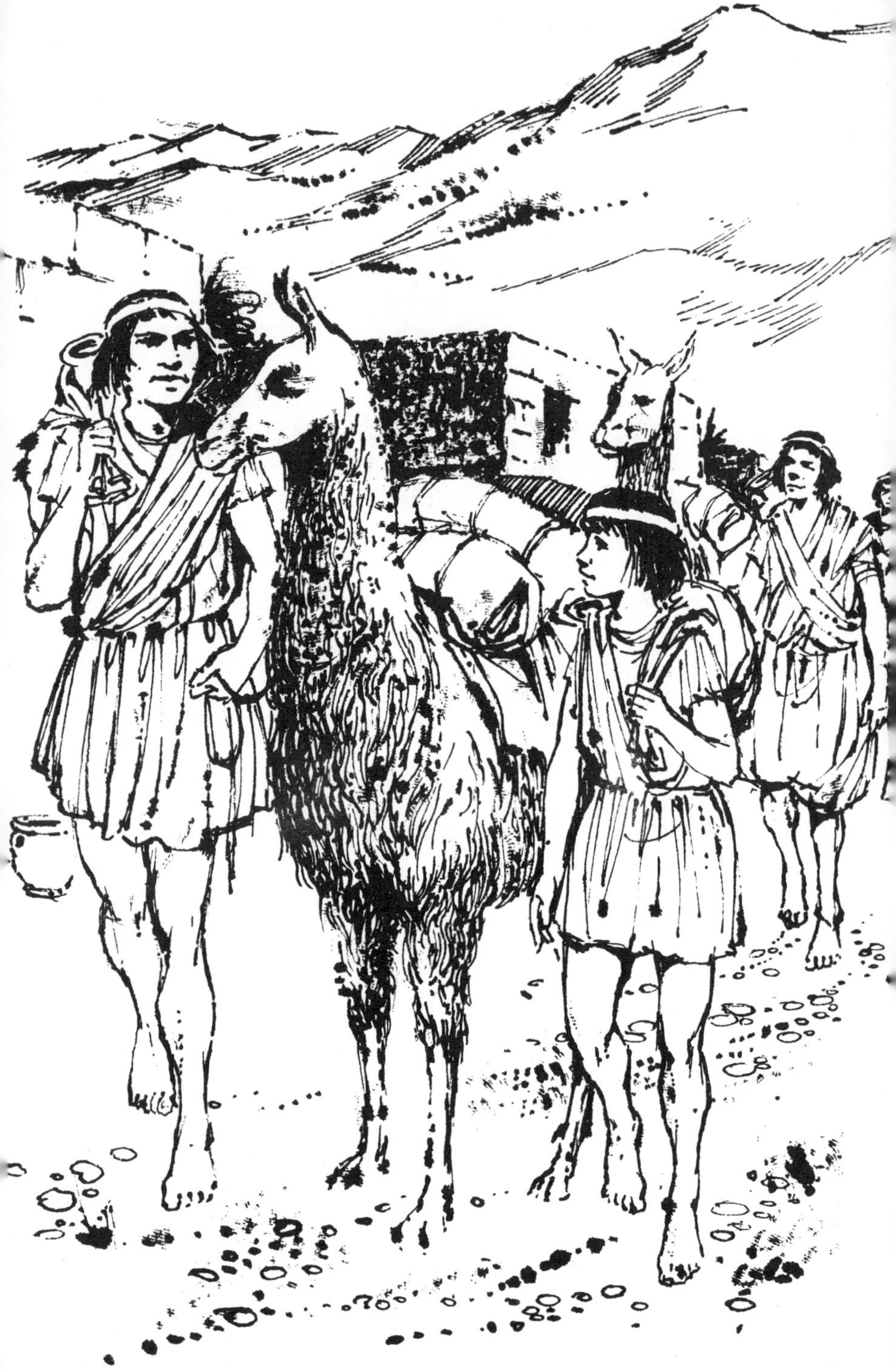

miles and packed them so tightly that there were not many spaces to be seen. They used their bronze knives to cut smaller stones to get into small spaces. Many times they had to grind these huge boulders with sand and water to get them to fit exactly. What wonderful builders they must have been. Their only tools were their bronze knives. Yet they built this beautiful temple of the sun. So tall that we can see the whole world from the top. I have never been to the top. Only specially chosen people go to the top. They say that you can see the vast ocean from there.

Many steps lead from the Holy Square to the top of the shrine. At this shrine the priest will offer gifts to our god, the Sun. After this offering, Sapa Inca will go to the garden of the temple and use the golden plough to turn the soil. This marks the beginning of the ploughing season. The garden of the Temple is a special one. In it are the best works of art of my people. Flowers, plants, shrubs, insects and vegetables of all sizes and varieties are made in gold. We believe that these golden plants and insects will encourage the earth to produce the best crops all year round.

Now the ceremony begins. The priests go up the steps, carrying a golden sun. It is followed by the chosen women and by the soldiers. After this there will be the great snake dance, performed in front of Sapa Inca. I must be there. Today is a special day. We are indeed happy.

1. Who were the Incas?
2. What do you think the ploughing season was? Why was it important to the Incas?
3. Why was Pacha happy?
4. How did Pacha's family get food and clothing?
5. Pacha's parents made many beautiful things. What are some of these things? Where can you see some of these things today?
6. What is a civilisation? Do you think the Incas were civilised?

19 The West Indian String of Pearls

God took pieces of a rainbow
And scattered them about
To form a necklace in the ocean
Linking North and South.

Then he blended all the colours
Of this string of pearls
Into trees and birds and flowers
Into happy boys and girls.

THELMA V. NORRIE

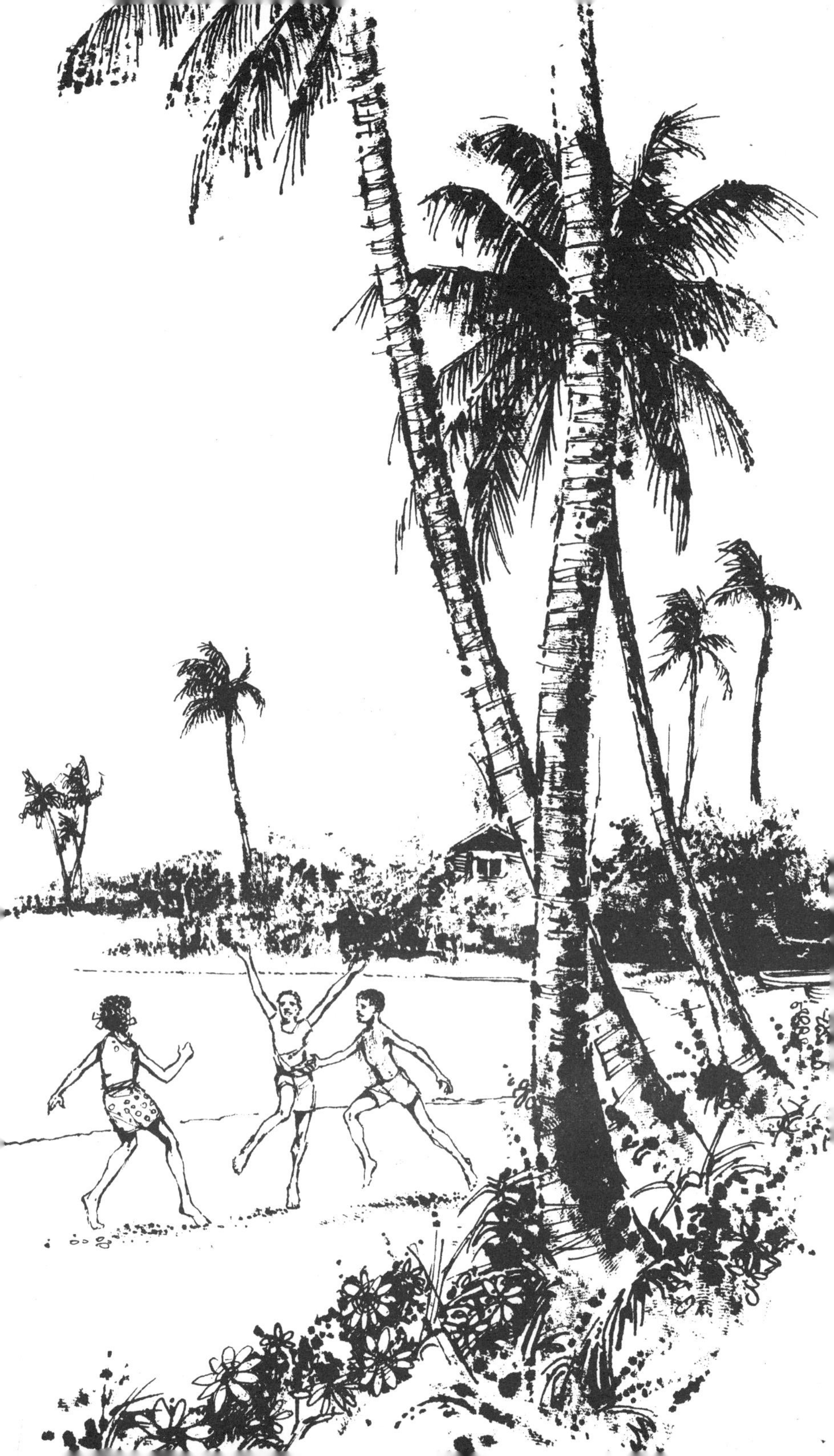

20 Humming Bird Makes It

We were pressing on at top speed, and on the 16th Fayal was only 390 miles away. When I relieved Kwai that evening, I found the wind increasing and the sky being rapidly overcast by banks of clouds. I figured they were the usual squalls and settled down in the cockpit, occasionally taking a bite from a chocolate bar. The squalls were soon tearing down on us. I quickly doused the mizzen and lashed it with a piece of cord. A steamer on the same course as ours, came up astern and took quite a long time to pass us, for we were travelling at about seven knots. *Humming Bird* was throwing up huge bow waves well above her decks.

It was no longer fun. Steering had become very difficult, and I could not hold my course. I finished my chocolate and shouted to the others to come on deck. Buck slept on in all that racket, oblivious to everything that was going on around him. I had to call him a few times before he awoke.

"Eh, what?" he stammered, realising that the ship was pitching like a wild pony.

"On deck, fast. We've got to get some sail off. Is Kwai up yet?"

"Coming," her reply floated up from the dark cabin.

She came up and steered, at the same time lighting the deck with our powerful flashlight, while Buck and I struggled with the sodden canvas, our hands numbed by cold spray. We soon had *Humming Bird* hove to, lying about 50 degrees to the wind and sea. She consequently rode the seas very well.

We found the weather had worsened after a night in our bunks. Great seas were hurtling towards us with the noise and impetus of express trains, as I staggered to the foredeck to change the medium jib for one of about 30 square feet. I had my nylon safety rope around my waist, with the other end clipped to a life line. The job took me almost an hour to complete. I was in the act of tightening a small shackle with a pair of pliers when a shout of "Watch out!" from Kwailan sent me scampering

'Humming Bird'

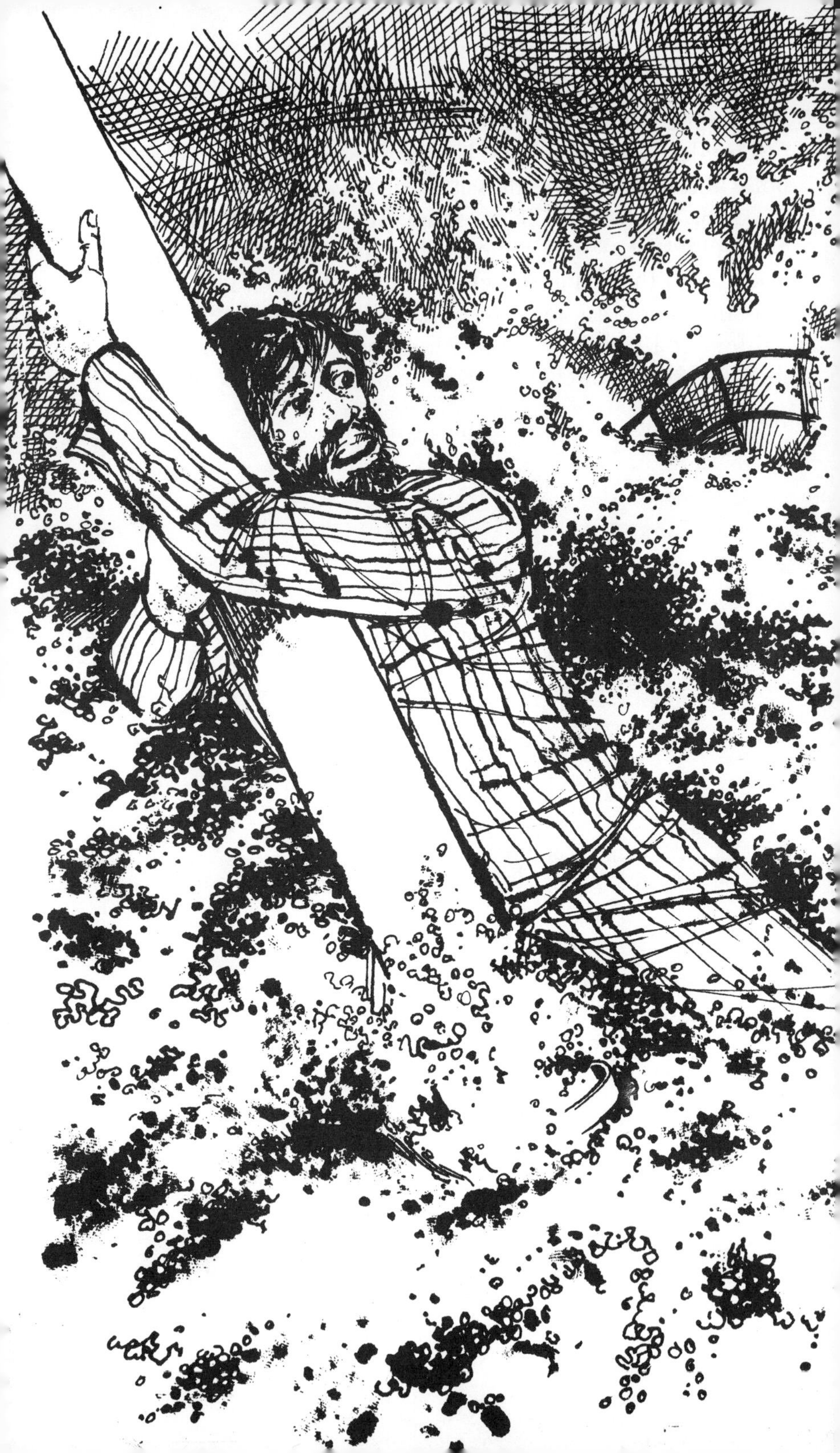

from the foredeck to grab hold of the mast. It seemed as if those huge combers would break on the bow. I eventually completed the job, hoisted the small sail and crawled aft on all fours. My pyjamas were soaking wet. I had forgotten to change them in the excitement.

I had always pictured gales as being accompanied by dark clouds and angry flashes of lightning. Conditions were totally different. The sun shone brightly, while white billowy clouds, their outlines hard against the steel blue of the sky, raced south-westward.

I lashed the tiller well to leeward. *Humming Bird* lay about five points off the wind, rising to almost every wave that threatened to engulf her. There was nothing left for us to do on deck except admire the grandeur of the scene. We had little desire to do this, for those waves, which were about twenty feet high, no longer needed to impress us that they were in deadly earnest.

We lay in our bunks all day trying to read and forget the weather outside. Occasionally a wave would break against the cabin sides, throwing tons of water over the top, and keeping us mindful of the strength of the elements with which we had dared to trifle.

Buck found the strength around noon to boil some rice and to heat up some corned beef and a tin of baked beans. Delicious. Half an hour later, Kwai and I were leaning over the side feeding the fish.

Buck, whose stomach must be made of cast iron, was filling up his plate with a second helping. The wind moderated at dusk and our spirits rose, but by nightfall it had returned to its full strength and kept us below for yet another night. We still kept watches, though, and looked out for steamers which might be bound for the Azores.

The gale was over by morning, but the seas were still running high. We set all sail and left *Humming Bird* to steer herself while we enjoyed a good breakfast. It was

18th June, my birthday. Kwailan was once more called upon to get out her recipes and down to the work only she could do. This resulted in sardine cakes fried in butter, white sauce, potatoes, even some blackeye peas, peanut punch, and custard and fruit for dessert.

Buck presented me with one of his new shirts, and Kwailan with the firm assurance that if we ever made land, she would cease to cook corned beef. I made a little speech, and informed my crew that Fayal was only 276 miles away.

I got some good sights on the 20th, putting us some 60 miles from Fayal—a distance shorter than that from Grenada to Trinidad. I continued to take sights all day to mark our progress. A plane flew overhead, but we could not see it through the clouds, and only heard its droning.

We saw two small motor vessels heading south at three o'clock and took them to be fishing boats. The water had taken on a different colour, changing from deep blue to dark green. Bits of weed and several birds appeared. I worked out we should sight the light on the south-western tip of Fayal around nine o'clock. The night was perfect for a landfall. A gentle breeze was blowing over the sea, and there was not a cloud in the sky.

Buck climbed the mast at about eight and peered ahead, but saw nothing. I took over from Kwailan at the tiller around nine and sent her below for a rest. My eyes soon adjusted themselves to the darkness, but my heart was beating like a triphammer.

"What if I'm wrong, and we are miles to the north or south of the island?"

I felt numb with fear and a dry taste came into my mouth. I saw visions of us approaching land, weeks after, in bad weather and not knowing where we were. We had no charts south of the English Channel. I went over

'Humming Bird' being built

in my mind again and again the method of working out sights. G.H.As., Azimuths, and Declinations swam before my eyes in a kaleidoscope, adding total confusion to my fear.

But what was that ahead? It could be a bright star just on the horizon. There it was again. I told myself that I must not excite the others, because it might be a ship. I left the tiller for a few moments and scrambled up the mast. *Humming Bird* rose on the top of a swell, and I saw the unmistakable blink of a lighthouse.

"My God!" I whispered. "We've made it!"

Then I was shouting, "Kwai! Buck! We've made it! THE LIGHT! I can see the LIGHT!" I nearly fell off my perch with excitement.

There was very little sleep for us that night, for we three stayed in the cockpit talking excitedly about our perfect landfall. It seemed incredible to us that by adding and subtracting a few figures in a certain order that we could have found this tiny island from almost 3,000 miles away. Anyway, we did not dwell too long on the miracle, but brought out a bottle of Muscatel and toasted each other until well past midnight.

We left Buck on deck steering for the next few hours, while we tried to get some sleep. I remember saying a silent prayer of thanksgiving before falling off. I thanked our Maker for bringing us safely all the way, and to the right place.

from AN OCEAN TO OURSELVES
by HAROLD LA BORDE

1. What is the effect of adding sail, and of reducing sail?
2. "Half an hour later, Kwailan and I were leaning over the side feeding the fish." What do you think this means?
3. The narrator appeared to be surprised at Buck's behaviour on two occasions. Which occasions are these?
4. 'The water had taken on a different colour, changing from deep blue to dark green, and bits of weed and several birds appeared'. What do you think these things indicated?
5. Find these words in your dictionary: mizzen, jib, tiller, hove-to, luff.

21 Marcus Garvey

Marcus Garvey was born near St Ann's Bay, Jamaica, on 17th August, 1887. He was the youngest of eleven children. His father was a mason by trade but there was never enough work for him, and never enough money for the family. Marcus' mother baked bread and cakes to earn extra money to feed the children, and Marcus delivered these cakes daily after school.

He left school when he was fourteen and was apprenticed to a printer. While he was learning the trade a dreadful hurricane struck Jamaica and his family lost all their possessions. So Marcus left St Ann's and went to Kingston where he found work in a printing office. He joined the Printers' Union and took an active part in trade union affairs.

Disaster struck again in January, 1907, when an earthquake shattered Kingston. The destruction and the fires which followed led to shortages of food and greatly increased prices. The Printers' Union struck for higher wages, but the strike was broken when the Union treasurer ran away with the funds. Most of the strikers returned to their jobs, but there was no job offered to Marcus Garvey. His former employers regarded him as a strike leader.

Eventually he found work at the Government printing office, and soon after this he started a newspaper which he called *The Watchman*. Its aims were to draw attention to the poverty of the working people, and to find means of improving their condition. The paper did not survive long and it closed down for lack of money.

During his years in Kingston Garvey saw much poverty. Always, it seemed, poverty and bad conditions were the lot of the black man. Garvey determined to devote all his energy to the cause of the Negro. He left Jamaica to travel in South America, and here he found Negroes living under conditions even worse than in his own country.

In 1912 he sailed for England, where he met students and seamen from India and Africa and learned about their countries. He came to the conclusion that the only way the Negro could be treated with the same respect as the white man was by gaining the independence of his native land. So it was that in 1914 he returned to Jamaica, more determined than ever to start a programme

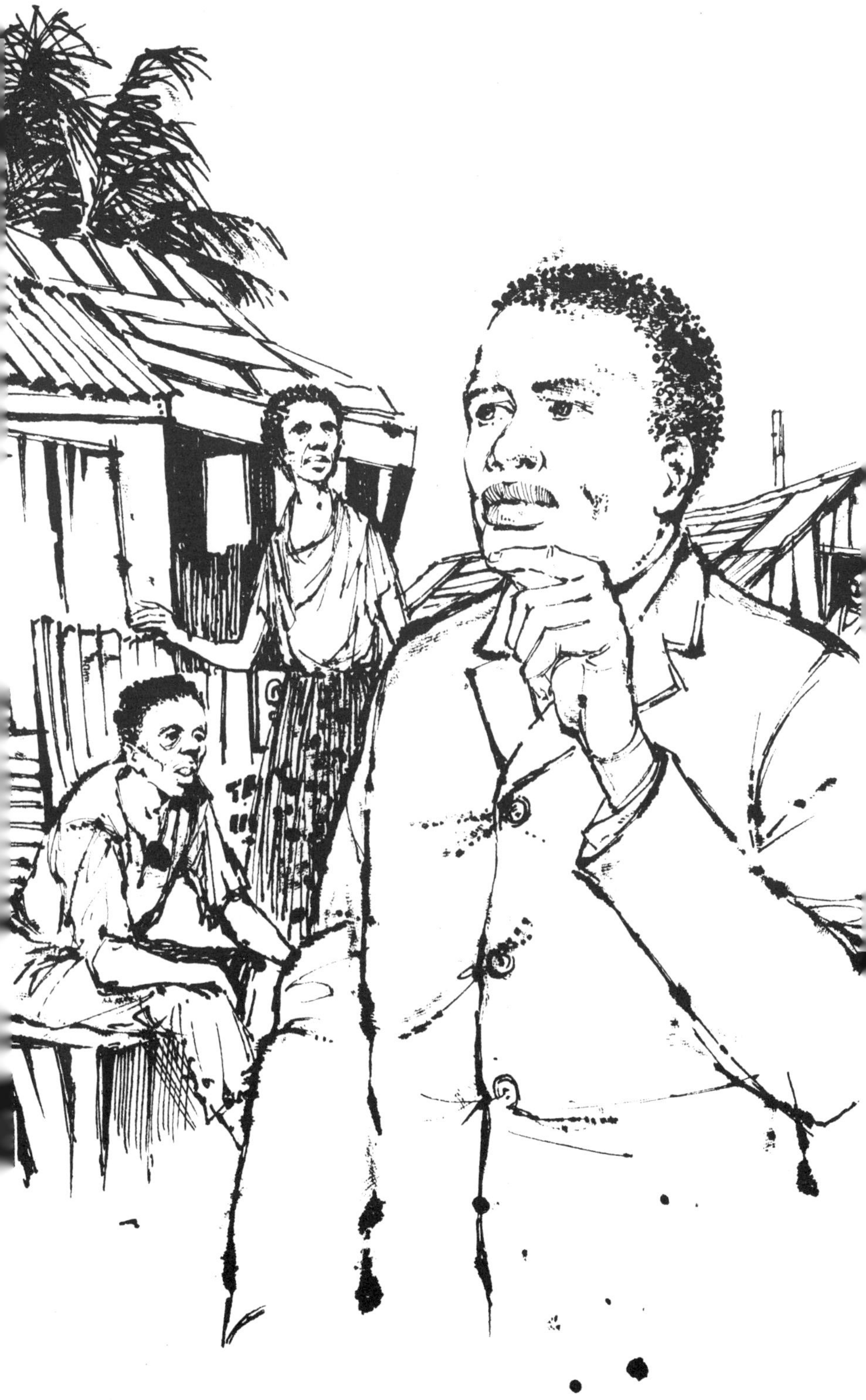

for the betterment of the Negro people of Jamaica and of the world.

He began by forming the Universal Negro Improvement Association (U.N.I.A.), which aimed to unite 'all the Negro people of the world into one great body to establish a country and Government absolutely their own'. He held meetings to increase the membership of his association, but the results were disappointing. He made enemies, too, for when he preached that Jamaica should be governed by black men he was charged with stirring up racial hatred.

Booker T. Washington, the great American Negro leader, invited Garvey to visit the United States. So in 1916 he left Jamaica for the third time, only to find the American Negroes living in conditions worse than those in his own country.

He made a decision. Since the black man, the Negro, was suffering so much in other lands the best thing for him to do was to go back to Africa, from which country he had been taken in the days of slavery. Marcus Garvey launched his Back to Africa plan by starting branches of the U.N.I.A. all over America. He toured the country, lecturing to enthusiastic crowds, and by 1919 his association claimed to have more than two million members. He encouraged Negroes to go into business, and set them an example by starting the Black Star Line, a shipping company with headquarters in New York. Only Negroes were allowed to contribute money to buy ships.

In August 1920 Garvey organised a great U.N.I.A. meeting in New York. It was attended by thousands of people including Negroes from many lands who came to hear his plans about going back to Africa. The meeting was a tremendous success for Garvey, and those who heard him speak gave their support to the Back to Africa movement. Shortly after the meeting arrangements were made with the President of Liberia, an African republic, for large numbers of Negro families to settle in his country.

But while plans for their resettlement were being discussed Garvey's Black Star Line began to run into problems. Three ships had been bought at a very high price, but one of these had been wrecked by the crew and now a second one had been seized by the port authorities. Garvey himself was warned by the Assistant District Attorney for New York for illegal practices. Shortly afterwards he was arrested for fraud and brought to trial. He was found guilty of selling stock in the Black Star Line when he knew the company to be bankrupt, and sentenced to five years imprisonment.

It was the end of Garvey's Back to Africa movement. In 1925 the Liberian Government reversed its earlier decision to allow the entry of Negro families.

Marcus Garvey served nearly three years of his sentence in Atlanta Federal Prison before being released and deported to his native land. He arrived in Kingston in December 1927 and was given a tremendous welcome by thousands of people. To them, he was their great hero. He had owned newspapers; he had managed factories; he had operated a shipping line, but—most important of all—he had campaigned successfully for the welfare and progress of the black man.

His stay in Jamaica was a short one. He left again to tour Central America and the other West Indian islands, lecturing to enthusiastic crowds which gathered to hear the great champion of the Negro cause. He carried the fight into Europe, holding large meetings in London and Paris. Finally, he returned to Jamaica to enter politics and to form the People's Political Party. Among its aims were self-government for Jamaica, higher wages, more employment, the establishment of a Jamaican university, and protection of the rights of the individual.

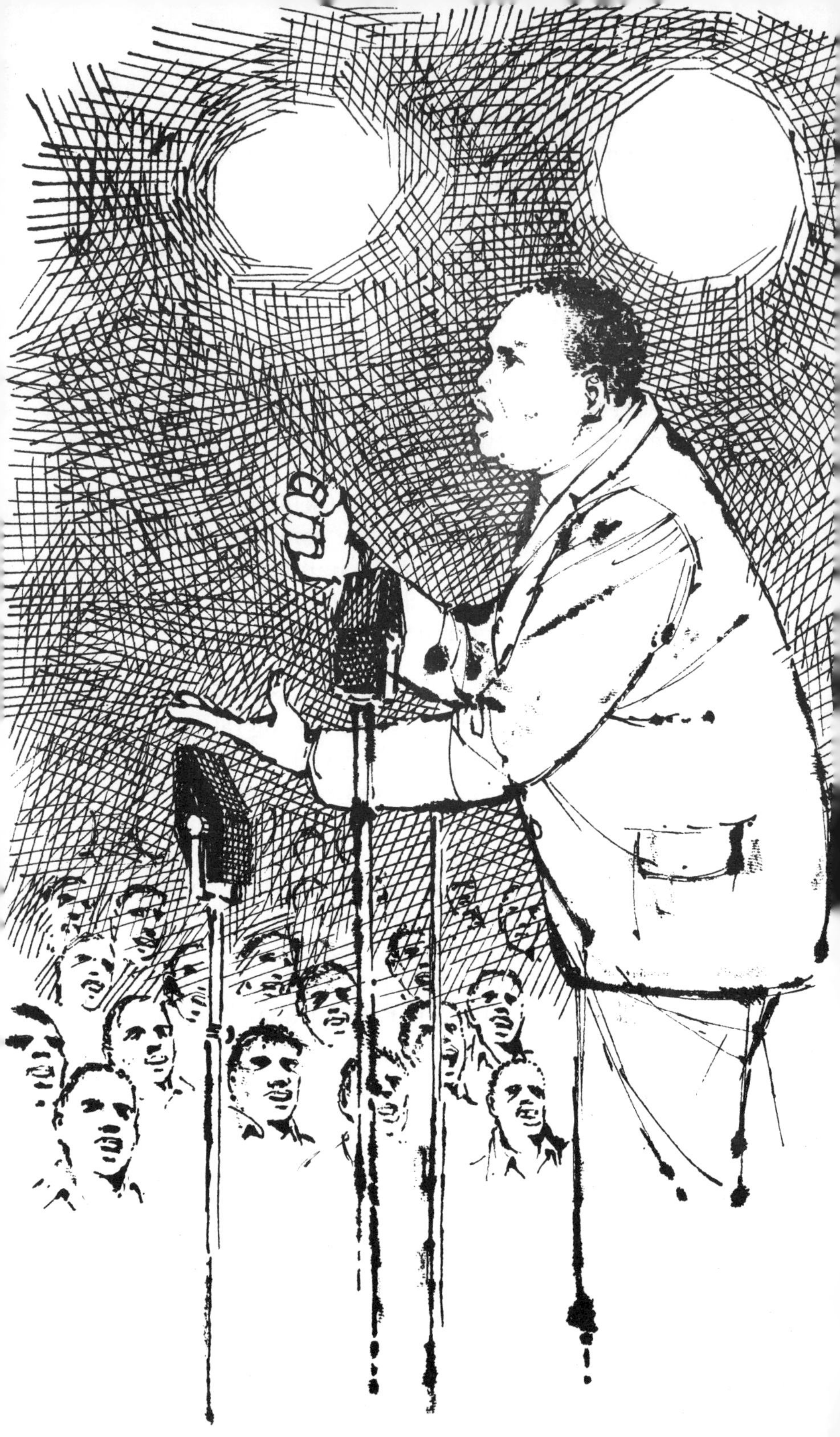

As usual, Garvey's fiery speeches delighted his followers, but in one speech he attacked the judges of the court. For this he went to jail for three months.

He was defeated in the elections of 1930, and though he continued to fight for the rights of the black man, he knew his political cause was lost. In 1935 he left Jamaica for the last time and sailed for England, feeling that it was pointless for him to fight on in Jamaica. Forgotten by his countrymen, he died in poverty in London in 1940.

But though he died alone, and far from his native land, Marcus Garvey's name is now honoured in Jamaica. In 1966 his remains were taken back to Jamaica and placed in a tomb in the George VI Memorial Park, and a bust of this great champion of the Negro marks his final resting place. He has since been proclaimed one of Jamaica's National Heroes.

from GREAT WEST INDIANS
by THÉRÈSE MILLS

1 What similarities were there in the careers of the young Garvey and the young Marryshow?
2 'Always, it seemed, poverty and bad conditions were the lot of the black man.' Try to find the exact meaning of the word 'lot'. The word 'lottery' may help you.
3 What did Garvey hope to achieve?
4 What is a strike? Show how it can at times be a good thing and at times a bad thing.
5 Say whether the following statements are true or false:
   (a) Marcus Garvey had eleven brothers and sisters.
   (b) Marcus Garvey had been taken from Africa in the days of slavery.
   (c) In 1925, the Liberian Government reversed its decision on the question of allowing black immigrants.
   (d) Garvey was deported to his native land where he died and was buried.

22 Market Women

Down from the hills they come,
With swinging hips, and steady stride,
To feed the hungry town.
They stirred the steep, dark land,
To place within the growing seed,
And in the rain and sunshine
Tended the young green plants.
They hoed, and dug and reaped,
And now, as Heaven has blessed their toil,
They come, bearing the fruits;
These handmaids of the Soil,
Who bring full baskets down,
To feed the hungry town.

DAISY MYRIE

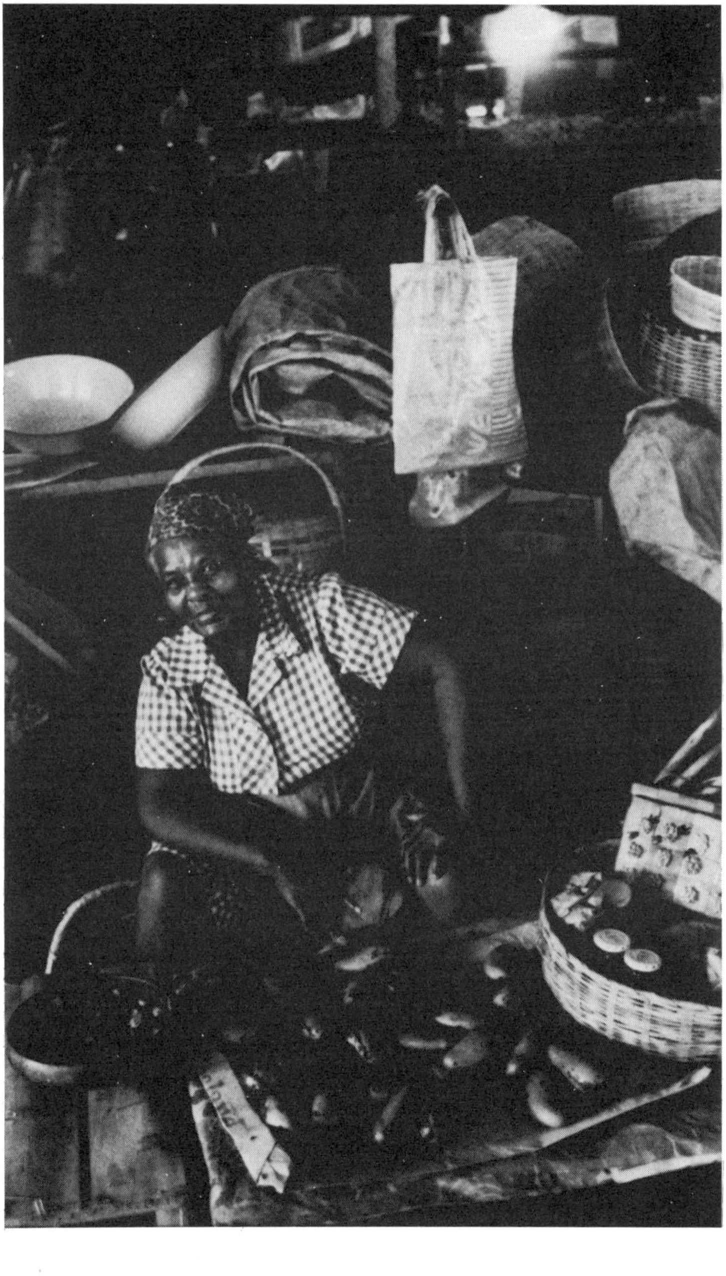

23 A Piper

A piper in the streets today
Set up, and tuned, and started to play
And away, away, away on the tide
Of his music we started; on every side
Doors and windows were opened wide
And men left down their work and came
And women with petticoats coloured like flame
And little bare feet that were blue with cold
Went dancing back to the age of gold.
And all the world went gay, went gay,
For half an hour in the street today.

SEUMAS O'SULLIVAN

24 An Exciting Test Match

The game began on the morning of Friday 9th December, 1960, at Brisbane, Australia. It was the first test match of the series between the home team and the West Indies. The West Indian captain, Frank Worrell, won the toss and decided to bat.

The Australians were favoured to win. Neil Harvey, Norman O'Neill, Richie Benaud, and Alan Davidson were all in the team and these were considered to be some of the finest cricketers in the world.

The West Indians, on the other hand, had not been having a particularly good tour. They had already been beaten twice and, in fact, had won only one first class game. It was true that in their team could be found talented players such as Kanhai, Sobers, Hunte, Ramadhin, and Worrell. But, somehow, the team had not yet 'clicked'. Many sports writers covering the tour criticised the West Indies' approach to the game. They felt that the West Indian batsmen in attempting to play bright cricket had been recklessly and foolishly throwing away their wickets. They thought that under these circumstances the West Indies stood no chance against the mighty Australians.

The West Indies scored 130 runs before lunch. This showed that they were continuing to play the game the West Indian way. For it was unusual for a team to score even a hundred runs before lunch in a test match. England, for example, had only scored 38 in this period at Brisbane in a previous series.

The hero of the West Indian innings was Gary Sobers, who scored a magnificent 132. Worrell and Solomon also played useful innings, each getting 65. At the end of the first day's play the West Indies had scored 359 runs for the loss of 7 wickets. On the second day, Alexander the wicket keeper fought his way to 60 and the fast bowler, Hall, hit out bravely for a quick 50. These two added 86 runs in an hour and enabled the West Indies to reach 453 made in 435 minutes. This was a fantastic run rate for a test match, especially against Australia.

Normally, the team that bats first in a test match and scores more than 400 runs places itself in an almost unassailable position. For not only is this total a difficult one to surpass, but even if the opposing team reaches it, there is hardly enough time left for either side to force a win.

Strangely enough, the West Indies could still be considered open to defeat for the simple reason that they had scored their runs too quickly. For here it was that after only ninety minutes play on the second day, Australia were about to bat, just as if the West Indians had been routed for a low score.

Australia, largely through the efforts of O'Neill, who scored 181, surpassed the West Indian total and, on the third day, were all out for 505, a lead of 52 runs. This left the game in an interesting position. A poor showing by the unpredictable West Indian batsmen in their second innings could easily leave Australia with a winning chance. As it was, the West Indies were bowled out for a modest score of 284 on the morning of the fifth day, leaving Australia to score 233 runs in 310 minutes for victory. Such a target was well within Australia's reach.

The West Indians took the field. Their trump card was the Barbadian, Wesley Hall. If he could capture a few quick wickets, anything might happen. But could Wes rise to the occasion? Or would this be one of his bad days when he would fail to find his best bowling form? The answers to these questions were not long in coming.

Hall had Simpson caught by Gibbs for a duck. Then Sobers threw himself full length to remove Harvey, again off Hall, and Australia were 7 runs for the loss of 2 wickets. The third wicket fell at 49, the fourth at the same score, and the fifth at 67. When the sixth wicket fell at 92, it began to look as if the West Indies would win handsomely.

But the Australians were not giving up without a fight. The all-rounders, Benaud and Davidson, were at the wicket and many felt that Australia, if these two survived, might be able to earn a draw.

Benaud and Davidson, however, had other ideas. With some fierce hitting, especially by the latter, and some almost suicidal short runs, they began to change the character of the game once again. Instead of merely trying to save the game, these two were trying to win it for Australia. To all appearances they were succeeding.

The West Indies needed a wicket badly. But nothing the skipper, Worrell, tried seemed to work. The gallant Australians continued to attack the bowling. With 45 minutes left, only 40 runs were needed. The Australians, who a short while ago were facing defeat were well on their way to victory.

With only 27 more runs needed, Worrell took the new ball and gave it to Hall for another spell. Could the big Barbadian succeed again? Or under the hot Australian sun was he a tired, demoralised man? If anything, the new ball brought an increase in the rate of scoring; 18 needed in 20 minutes, 11 needed in 16 minutes, 10 needed in 15 minutes. . . .

Now Sobers bowls to Benaud as Australia require nine more runs. The Australian spectators after so many anxious moments are now in their glee. It is only a matter of time. Benaud plays the fourth ball of the over to square leg and starts to run. Solomon hits the wicket with a direct throw and Davidson is run out by yards. The partnership has been broken, at last! At the end of Sobers' over, with Benaud and Grout at the wicket, Australia still require six runs with three wickets to fall.

Hall begins to bowl the last over of the day. The first delivery strikes Grout on the hip. But even as he is about to double over in pain, Benaud calls him for a run. No opportunity can be wasted. Then Benaud tries for a big hit off a bouncer and is caught by Alexander for 58. Five runs are needed, two wickets to fall, six balls to be bowled.

Meckiff, the new batsman, plays the first of these quietly back to the bowler. He misses the next one, but they are able to run a bye. Hall bowls and Grout hits the ball in the air in the direction of square leg. Groans come from the crowd. It is going to be an easy catch.

But Hall, in a state of excitement, apparently forgets that there are other fieldsmen on the ground. Never once taking his eyes off the ball, he continues running to get under it and collides with Kanhai who had been waiting to take the catch. The ball falls harmlessly to the ground and the batsmen take a single.

Three runs are now needed for victory. Hall bowls to Meckiff who hits the ball over Hunte's head towards the square leg boundary. A four would end everything. Hunte gives chase. The batsmen, having run two are already on their third run, when Hunte pounces on the ball and from the boundary, throws it straight into Alexander's gloves, inches from the bails. Grout is run out!

But the two completed runs still count. The scores are now tied. Only a single is needed as the last man, Kline, comes in to face Hall. Kline plays the ball and the batsmen dash off for the single that would mean victory. Solomon races in, picks up the ball with one hand, and for the second time in the innings, hits the stumps with a direct throw. Meckiff is run out. The game is over. A tie is the result. The spectators storm the field to congratulate the players. Nobody on that Brisbane ground had ever seen or could hope to see a more exciting match. Everybody agrees that neither team deserved to lose it.

The performance by the two teams injected new life into the dying game called cricket. Only 5,000 people had witnessed the last day's play in that memorable match. But by the time the tour was over, 500,000 Australians lined the streets to cheer the West Indians.

1. Why is the Australian team referred to as the 'home team'? When is the West Indian team called the 'home team'?
2. What is meant by 'the team had not yet clicked'?
3. At what points in the game might the West Indians have considered themselves safe from defeat?
4. People in the West Indies have to listen to cricket broadcasts from Australia during the night. Why is this so?
5. When a bowler bowls three overs in Australia, how many balls has he bowled?

Sir Learie with his wife, Norma, and daughter, Gloria, in 1933

25 Learie Constantine

The dedication in Learie's book *Cricket in the Sun* reads thus:

> To
> MY WIFE
> Who has a husband in winter
> But who has been comrade, adviser, and inspiration
> summer and winter alike

This sums up briefly the pattern of Learie Constantine's family life over a number of years. Norma, his wife, and Gloria, his daughter, had learned to live without his physical presence for the greater part of each year.

Prior to her marriage to Learie, Norma Cox, as she was then, had found it difficult to "play second fiddle" to cricket. She lived in the city. Learie lived in the country, and worked in Port of Spain. He travelled to and from work by train, and the last train left the city at 7 p.m. On evenings after work, Learie would hurry to the nets to practise for as long as possible. The longer he practised, the less time it left for him to spend with Norma before he had to hurry off to catch the train home.

Things went on like this for a time, until Norma felt that she could tolerate the situation no longer. She issued an ultimatum to Learie.

"Make your choice! It's either cricket or me!"

He pleaded earnestly with her.

"Don't make it difficult for me," he begged. "Please let it be cricket *and* you. I don't want to give up either."

Looking back on those days, Norma often smiled at the memory of how completely bowled over she had been by his request. She had acquiesced. Instead of allowing herself to feel jealous, she began to take a keener interest in his cricket. She and Learie were eventually married on the 25th of July, 1927.

"You'll never regret this," he promised. She never did.

When Learie went to Lancashire in 1929 to take up his first appointment as professional with the Nelson Cricket Club, Norma accompanied him, but their infant daughter was left behind in Trinidad with her grandparents.

The difficulties of those early months, when as strangers in Nelson they had no one else but each other to turn to for company or comfort, served more than anything else to draw them closer together in a bond which was never afterwards broken. It was a long time before any neighbour even looked through a window to exchange "Good-morning" with them. When he left the cricket field, Norma was all that Learie had.

With her he shared the funny side of life. In the early days she had been amused by his seemingly serious assertion that on many an occasion he had bowled an English cricketer out, and the latter had walked to the pavilion and turned and walked straight back out to the wicket again. Englishmen had seemed all alike to him!

It was to Norma, too, that he poured out his doubts and fears, his joys and sorrows. She became his source of strength. When he was despondent, it was she who cheered him up. He always attributed to her the fact that he stayed on in Nelson after their first two years there.

Often he received abusive letters, asking him why he did not go back to his own country; and these letters made him sad. In this unhappy situation, Norma had enjoined, "Let us turn and fight it. In the end they will realise that basically we are just like them, and they will accept us in spite of our colour." Her words proved true.

C. L. R. James, in his book *Beyond a Boundary* was able to relate an incident which bore testimony to the fact that by 1932 the Constantine family had been recognised as citizens of Nelson.

During the time that James stayed at the home of Learie and Norma, a friend turned up one morning for a chat and a cup of tea. As she was leaving, she turned to Norma and said that she was just going to do her own shopping, and that she would be willing to do Norma's too, if the latter had not yet done it.

Some time after the friend had left, Learie pointed out to James what a nasty day it was outside. "Her offer to do Norma's shopping," he explained, "was just to save Norma from going out on a day like this. That is really why she came."

The Constantines had at last been drawn into the circle.

Learie's return to the West Indies after his first stint as professional at Nelson was followed by an invitation to play cricket in New York. This tour was organised by a group of West Indians living in New York. Norma was invited to accompany him. At the end of the engagement, Learie received an honorarium, but he took back with him also the memory of a wonderful catch which he had made in one match, and the resulting swarming of the pitch by spectators who rained coins and notes upon him. Norma was silent when she saw in his eyes the look that indicated that he was trying to shut out the memory of something less spectacular, but could she blame him? After having been advertised as "the fastest bowler in the world, and a harder hitter than Gilbert Jessop," it must have been a blow to his pride to have scored 1 in his first innings and 4 in his second. But such are the ups and downs of cricket!

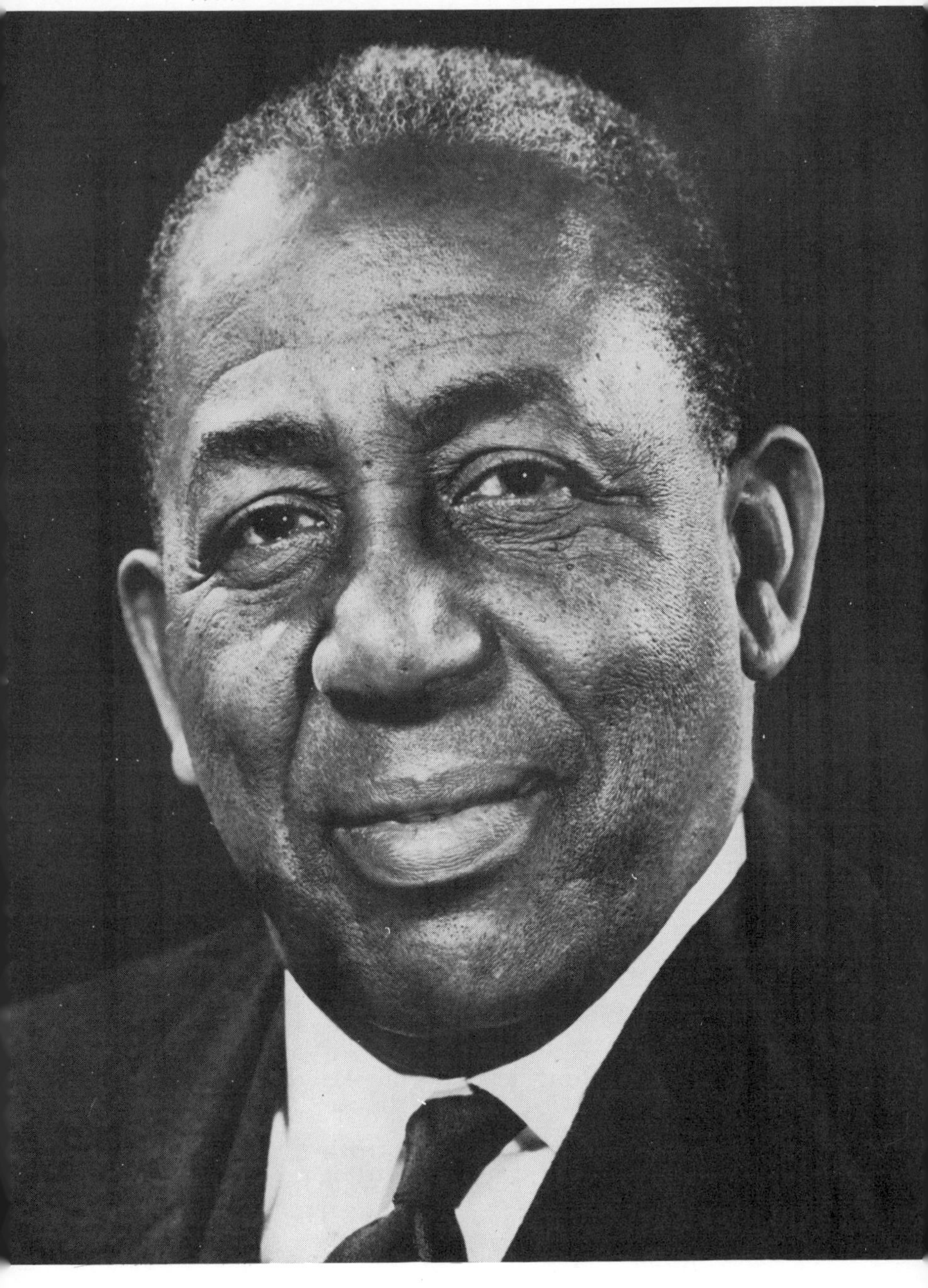

When Learie went back to Nelson for his second season, little Gloria accompanied her parents. The family was now complete. Years before, Learie had visualised himself coaching a son of his at cricket, just as his father had coached him, but this was never to be. Gloria remained their only child. If Learie did not have the privilege of seeing a son of his play cricket, at least his daughter as she grew up, had the pleasure of watching him, and feeling proud of his achievements, for Norma always took Gloria along to see all the big matches in which her father played.

from A LOOK AT LEARIE CONSTANTINE
by UNDINE GIUSEPPI

1 Why did Learie Constantine go to live in Nelson?
2 In what ways did his wife help him to settle in Nelson?
3 Was Constantine's tour of New York a success for him? Why?
4 What made the Constantines favourites of the people of Nelson?
5 How did little Gloria get along in Nelson?

26 Port Royal — City of Silence

When, in 1494, Christopher Columbus sailed along the southern coast of Jamaica he was struck not only by the verdant hills in the distance, but also by the almost completely sheltered natural harbour around which present-day Kingston is built. Four and a half centuries ago there were a number of sandy cays[1] stretching across the mouth of this harbour. The largest of these, Cayo de Carena, was subsequently used by the Spaniards for careening[2] their ships on the way to and from the lucrative coasts of Central America.

One hundred and fifty years later Cagway, a corruption of the original name, had developed into a bustling township catering to settlers who had established the island's capital—San Jago de la Vega (now Spanish Town)—some distance away inland. In 1655, the English captured the island and soon afterwards encouraged the 'buccaneers'—so called because of their custom of smoke-curing meat over small fires called *boucans*—to transfer their headquarters from Tortuga (off Haiti) to Cagway.

In a short time these buccaneers had made the town their base of operations for harassing the King's enemies on the sea. In this they were encouraged by 'letters-of-marque' issued by the English Crown, and their very ferociousness and presence guaranteed the defence of the island from any retaliation.

One day in June 1616 crowds were seen hurrying towards the docks. A hum of excitement pervaded the air. One name was carried on all lips: "Commodore Myngs", whose ship had just dropped anchor off Cagway.

Commodore Myngs' treasure was the first big booty brought to the island and was estimated to contain at least 1,500,000 pieces-of-eight. A contemporary wrote that "there is not one man on this island but received

[1] cay: small island of coral or sand.
[2] careen: to turn (ship) over for cleaning and caulking.

some benefit of that action." By this time the shallow waters that divided the cays from the mainland had been filled in. The whole narrow strip is known as the 'Palisadoes'.

When the English took Jamaica from the Spanish, Cagway changed its name to Port Royal. Men and women came from inland to earn a living by supplying services to the pirates, buccaneers, traders and others who came to the port. Although in 1668 the boisterous town counted 8,000 souls, there were complaints from the more sober-minded that "there is not now resident upon this place ten men to every house that selleth strong liquors." Port Royal then ranked with Santo Domingo, Havana, and Panama City as one of the four largest cities in the Caribbean.

Most famous among the loose-living buccaneers was Henry Morgan, a young Welshman who had been elected 'Admiral' of the Brethren of the Coast. After attacking Puerto Principe (now Camaguey) in Cuba in 1668, Morgan arrived in Port Royal with the looted treasure. His share of the spoils was believed to have been 50,000 pieces-of-eight. To this day it is still unaccounted for.

Under the Treaty of Madrid signed in 1670, the English agreed to suppress the buccaneers in exchange for Spanish recognition of their capture of Jamaica.

But before the end of the year, Morgan broke the treaty by sacking Panama of over 750,000 pieces-of-eight. Both he and the Governor of the island, Sir Thomas Modyford, were arrested and taken to London. King Charles II took a liking to Morgan, and appeased the Spanish by putting all the blame for the exploit on Sir Thomas, whom he divested of his office and sent to the Tower. Morgan was later knighted and returned to Jamaica as Lieutenant Governor, Chief Judge of the Admiralty Court and Custos of Port Royal. He died

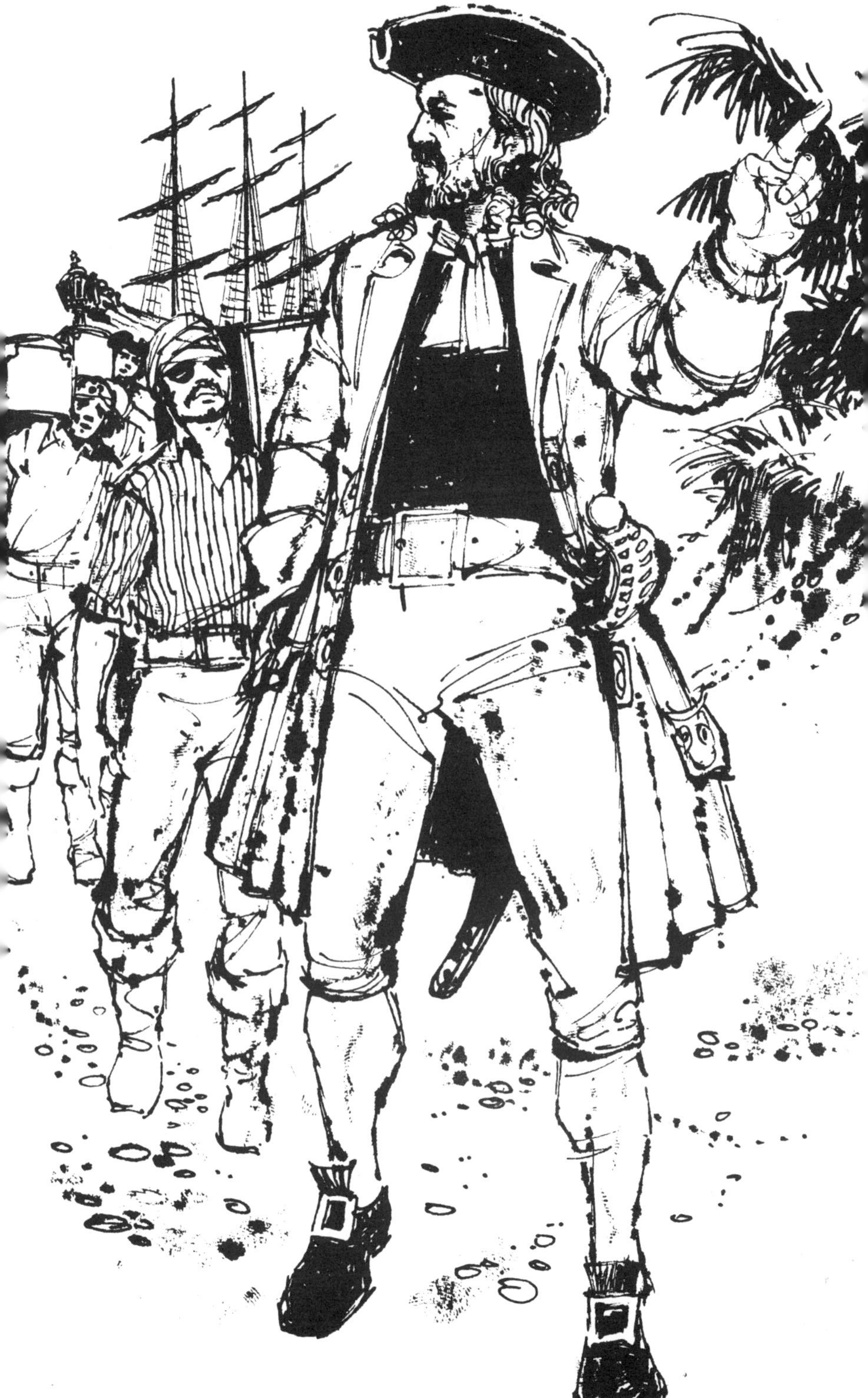

from excessive drinking in 1688.

Four years later the Day of Judgment, predicted for years by the pious, befell Port Royal. Writing about the fatal 7th June, 1692, Dr Heath, Rector of the city, tells of having a pre-dinner drink of wormwood wine with the acting governor before going to the house of Captain Ruben, his host for the evening. ". . . I found the ground rolling and moving under my feet, upon which I asked, 'Lord, sir, what is this?' He replied, being a very brave man, 'It is an earthquake; be not afraid, it will soon be over.'" Dr Heath also recounts that on going towards Morgan's Fort he saw the earth open and "swallow up a multitude of people."

Houses fell, wide cracks opened up in the earth, ships were torn from their moorings and drifted out to sea, more than half the land sank, taking with it most of the town—buildings, streets, people, hidden treasure. When the clouds of dust settled there was only the wailing of the survivors to break the terrifying silence that followed.

When the Treaty of Utrecht at the end of the War of the Spanish Succession gave the English complete control of the buying and selling of African slaves to Spanish America, the new town of Kingston became the slave centre of the New World. Commercial activity on the island shifted from Port Royal to Kingston and although there have been many attempts to resettle the cay, except for a handful of hardy fisher-folk living in dilapidated houses along narrow streets, today there is nothing to awaken the visitor's interest on land. But beneath the waves . . .

In the miraculously preserved outline, ten fathoms deep, in waters that sparkle in tropic sunlight rests Port Royal—a city of silence. Over the centuries polyps have coated the buildings with coral magic. Silently, multicoloured fish drift in and out of doorways, cruise along forgotten streets and passageways. Here, a church,

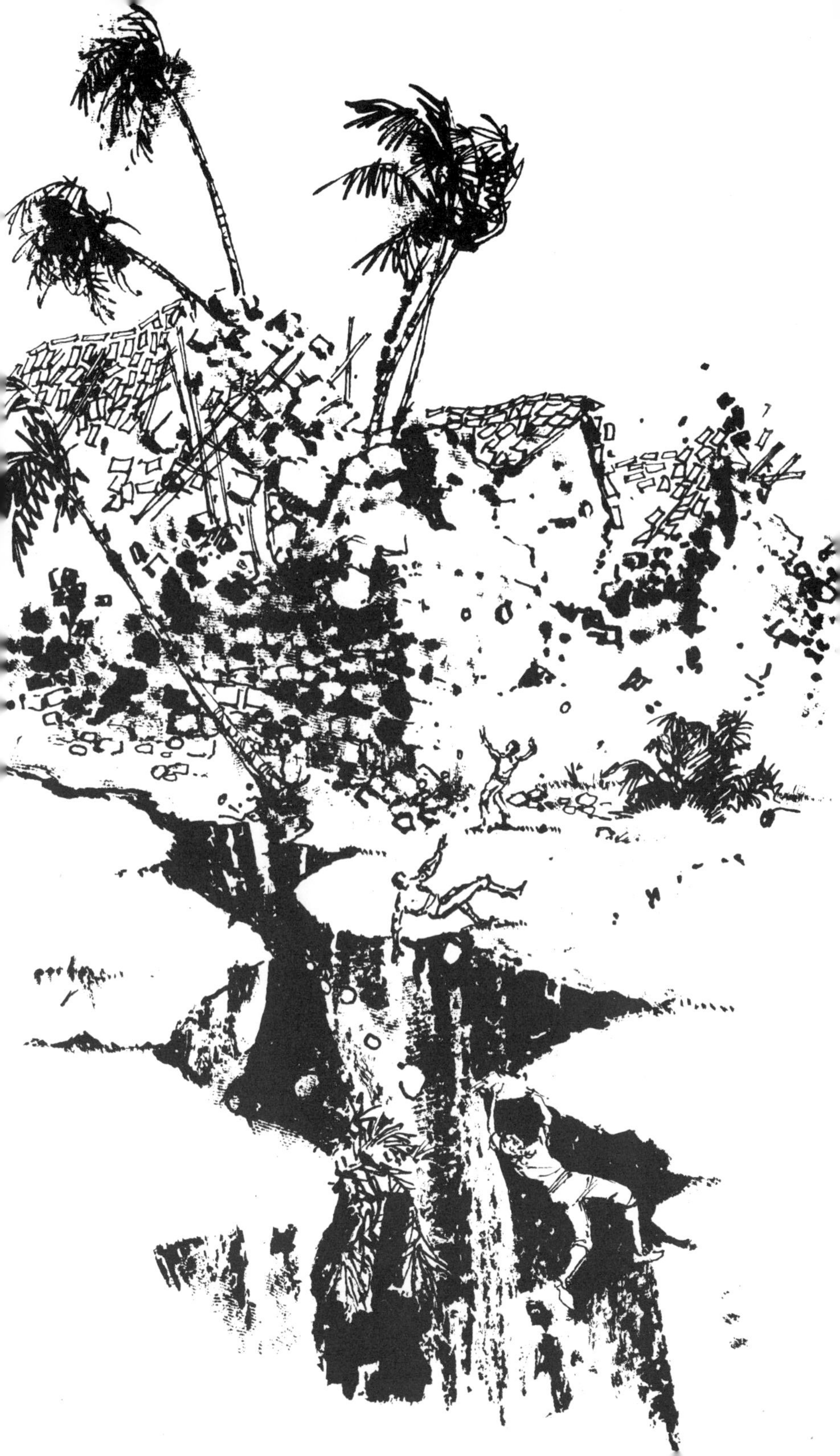

its creamy lustre in stark contrast with the reds and blues of a garden of coral stalagmites; there, coral fronds fan a welcome to visitors who peer through glass-bottomed boats from above.

Port Royal has become the happy hunting ground of skin divers, underwater photographers and treasure hunters. The never-ceasing play of water filtered sunlight on silent buildings presents an uncanny, ever-changing kaleidoscope of colour—always an interesting topic in the conversation of disappointed but happily tired searchers for the fabulous 'Morgan's Treasure'.

U.N.E.S.C.O. FEATURES

1   Find out if there are any towns or villages in your country which carry Spanish names.
2   'There is not now resident upon this place ten men to every house that selleth strong liquours.' Does this sentence mean that there were too many liquour shops or too few?
3   Why did the pious people predict that Port Royal would be destroyed?
4   Find out what you can about the buccaneers.
5   Say whether the following statements are *true* or *false*:
    (a) It may still be possible to find Morgan's treasure.
    (b) Magic was responsible for the destruction of Port Royal.
    (c) Not one man on the island received any benefit from Commodore Myngs' treasure.
    (d) Dr Heath destroyed Port Royal.

27 June

Trinidad in June
And the little Island yonder
Settling!
Ah goodness,
These in June
In morning twilight time;
These in June
When winds on doves' feet walk
And sun is high;
These in June
On golden afternoons,
Make a real world.
The mason whistles by the wall,
The digger sings.
The washer dances to a beating tune
Beggars are kings.

           HAROLD M. TELEMAQUE

28   Ra II Arrives in Barbados

On July 8 we were only 200 nautical miles from Barbados, and the authorities sent a fast little government boat, the *Culpepper*, to welcome us to this little independent corner of the British Empire. Yvonne and our eldest daughter, Annette, were the only passengers on board.

Ra II at sea

If they found us on the basis of our position we should meet late that same night.

The night passed, and the day as well, while the *Culpepper* rolled about, over and among the waves of our immediate neighbourhood, without finding us. The weather was far from perfect and we intercepted reports from the government boat to the land station describing the big waves and reporting that the raft sailor's wife was suffering from seasickness but bravely insisted on continuing the search. The search went on for two more nights and two more days. It was near nightfall on the second day and we half expected to reach land before the government boat, for there were barely a hundred nautical miles left. Then the *Culpepper* appeared, also on the wrong horizon, overtaking us from astern. Flat and broad and seaworthy, a real man's boat, she manoeuvred alongside, with two white women clinging to the railings, surrounded by a waving black crew. While the ladies were obviously having difficulty in sorting out all the sunburned shaggy creatures with full beards, waving wildly from the roof of the wicker cabin, the crew of the *Culpepper* turned their attention to Madani, whom they thought to be a sailor from Barbados. Madani, the landlubber from Marrakesh, impressed the onlookers by throwing out a fishhook baited with salt sausage and immediately pulling in five pampano and an unknown silver-green fish of the same general type. Georges, the skin diver, crossed to the *Culpepper* just as the sun was setting to negotiate a morally permissible barter: fresh fish, Egyptian bread and the ever tasty Moroccan *sello* in exchange for unnecessary but very welcome oranges. He was standing on the afterdeck, about to dive for his swim back to *Ra II* with the *Culpepper's* searchlight playing on the waves to show him the way, when a black man stopped him and asked him if we on *Ra* were not afraid of sharks.

"No," said Georges grandly, but swallowed his boast when the man pointed calmly to a large man-eater, gliding slowly out of the ship's wake into the beam of light. Our own rubber raft was so worn by rubbing against the earthenware jars on board that we did not dare to launch it. Georges had to spend the night on the *Culpepper* and return next morning in a little oarless dinghy let out on tow from the *Culpepper*, and hauled back again empty.

The *Culpepper* stayed on our port quarter all night. The day after, 12th July, such large flocks of sea birds flew out toward us from the west that we knew land must be just over the horizon. It was Sunday, and Norman and I, who had the five to eight watch, were standing on the bridge looking forward to our relief. Soon Carlo and Kei would be scrambling out and unbedding our last eggs from the lime paste to be fried for the occasion: Sunday breakfast. We still had plenty of provisions, especially sacks of Eyptian mummy bread in the chests we slept on, salt sausage and ham hanging under the wicker roof, and jars of *sello*, the honey and almond mixture that contained everything a desert traveller in Morocco needed. We had never gone hungry and were in good form. Then I noticed something and grabbed Norman by the arm.

"Do you smell it?" I said, sniffing up the salt sea air. "Fantastic, a distinct scent of green, fresh-cut grass!"

The two of us stood and sniffed. We had been at sea for fifty-seven days. Santiago, Carlo and the others came out and sniffed with us. The non-smokers among us smelt it distinctly. And damned if I didn't scent cow dung, as well, the smell of farming. It was pitch dark and we could see nothing. But the movement of the waves was strange too, a different rhythm, somehow, which must be the effect of backwash from land. We pushed both rudder-oars hard over to starboard, where

Thor Heyerdahl

the wind was coming from, and held a course as close to the north as we could. It was incredible how well the low-lying reed boat was able to sail close-hauled.

Norman, Carlo and Santiago climbed to the masthead in turn all morning, and at twelve-fifteen our time we heard a wild yell from above our heads:

"Hurrah!"

Norman had sighted land. Safi screamed and the duck flapped across the roof. Like flies we swarmed up the steps of the swaying masts, every man jack of us, for *Ra II* was incredibly stable, now that most of the papyrus was under water. The *Culpepper* blew her siren. Then we all saw land, low and flat on the horizon to the northwest. We had steered too far south the day before, trying to counteract the current that swung north just before the islands. We had succeeded only too well. So now we had to turn the mainsail and shove the rudder-oars right over in the opposite direction, otherwise we would sail past Barbados and land somewhere on the dense chain of islands just behind. That was all very well, but family and friends were by now waiting for us on Barbados. *Ra II* responded to manoeuvering like a keeled vessel. The straight deep furrow running right along the bottom between the two reed rolls evidently acted as a negative keel. With the wind almost across our beam the red life buoy was being towed dead astern, showing that we were moving in the direction the bow was pointing, without any side drift, straight towards the low coastline.

When we sat down round the poultry coop for lunch we knew it would be our last meal on board. Late in the afternoon we heard the hum of aircraft. A little private plane circled over us, leaning from side to side in greeting. Soon after, a bigger, twin-engined plane came out from the islands with the Prime Minister of Barbados, and soon there were four planes circling over our mast top.

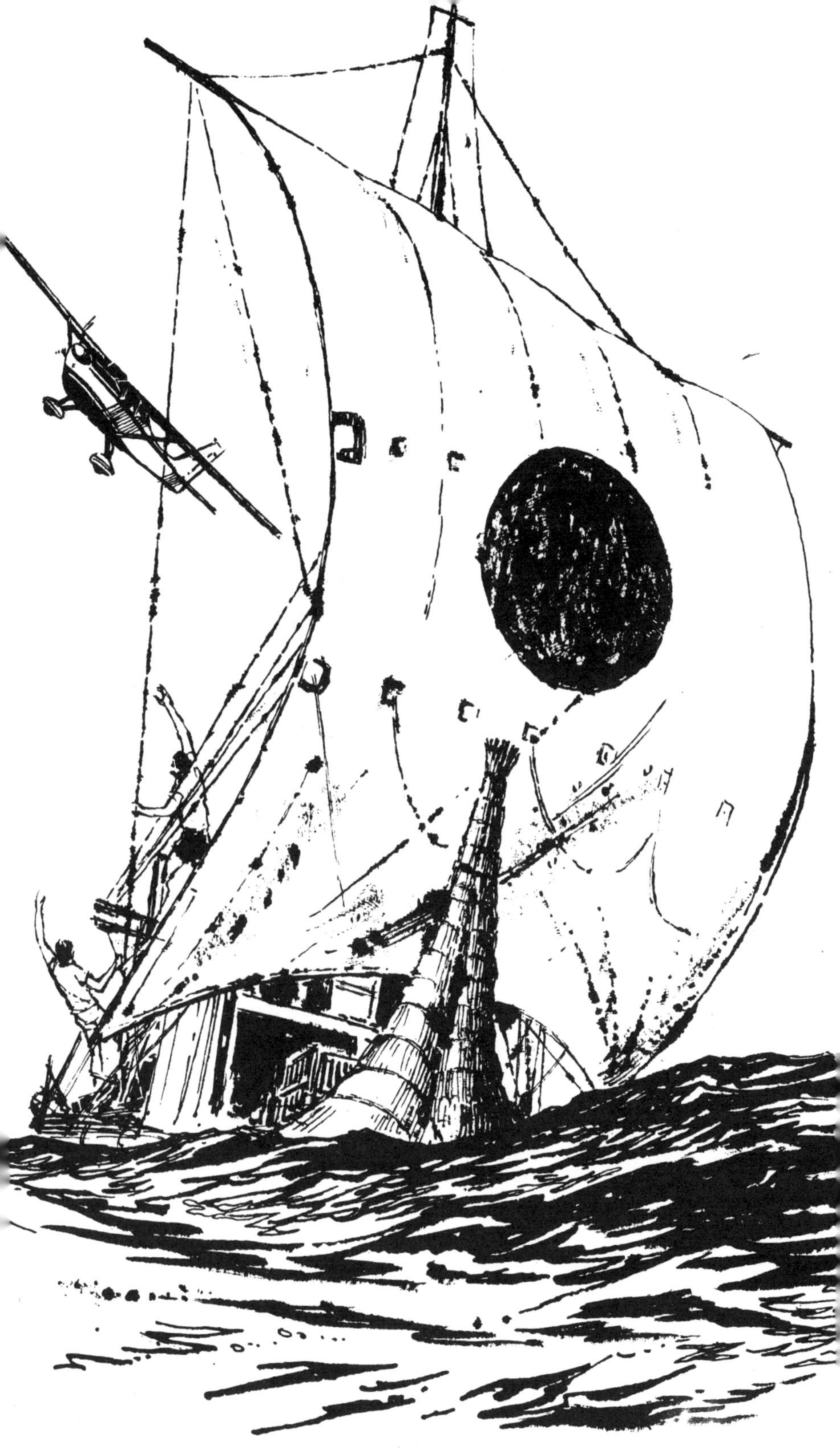

One of them dived so low that its slip stream threatened to take the mainsail aback. The land mass rose higher and the sun flashed on the glass of distant windows. We saw more and more houses. Dozens of boats were on their way out through the land haze. A speedboat came bucking over the waves with Norman's wife, Mary Ann, and my two youngest daughters, Marian and Bettina, on board. Boats of all sorts. Seasick faces, joyful faces, gaping faces. Some were laughing themselves silly, shouting and asking if we had really come from Morocco on "that thing". Seen from outside, we were just a wickerwork cabin floating on the water behind a majestic Egyptian sail, with two shorn-off tufts of reed sticking out of the water at either end.

Yuri's motley rag curtain did not exactly reinforce the impression of an ocean voyager either. Over fifty vessels of every type and size finally escorted *Ra II* across the finishing line. We were making for Bridgetown, the capital. Sailboats, speedboats, fishing boats, yachts of many kinds, a catamaran, a trimaran, a police boat, a Hollywood-type full-rigger decorated as a pirate ship and packed with tourists, and our old friend the *Culpepper*, circled round us in a mêlée that made the peace-loving Carlo long for the solitude of the sea. Georges, on the other hand, felt quite at home; he lit our last red flare and installed himself like the Statue of Liberty on the cabin roof.

So ended the voyages of *Ra*. Outside Bridgetown harbour we lowered the bleached mainsail with its round solar orb for the last time, and furled it while the crew of the *Culpepper* tossed us a tow rope.

The harbour area was swarming like an anthill. Every street was packed with people. It was five minutes to seven p.m. by our watches; we had to adjust them to Barbados time, a long awaited moment, for we had sailed 3,270 nautical miles, or more than 6,100 kilo-

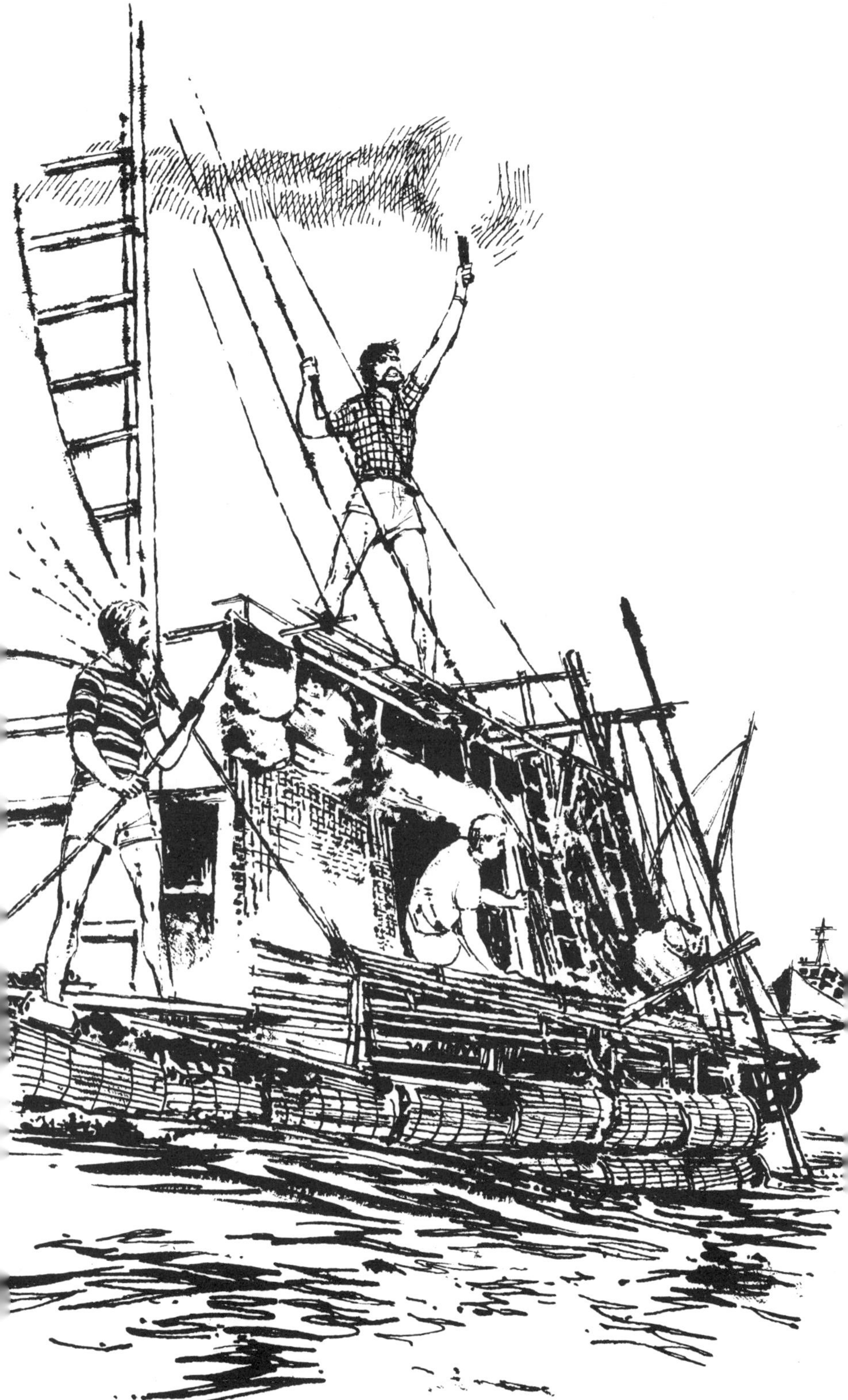

metres, since we last set foot on land.

Before putting into the quay we found an opportunity to shake hands, all eight of us. There was no one of us who failed to realise that it was only thanks to a common effort that we had come safely across the sea.

from RA II
by THOR HEYERDAHL

1　In what way was *Ra II* different from other boats?
2　In what way was the behaviour of the crew of *Ra II* similar to that of the crew of *Humming Bird* when land was sighted?
3　How many people were on board *Ra II*?
4　In the final sentence, the narrator suggests that good co-operation was responsible for the successful voyage. In what other story in this book are we told that good co-operation was important to success?
5　Find out if the full story of the *Ra* expedition is in your school library or the Public Library in your county. If it is available, be sure to read it.

29 A Sad Song about Greenwich Village

She lives in a garret
   Up a haunted stair,
And even when she's frightened
   There's nobody to care.

She cooks so small a dinner
   She dines on the smell,
And even if she's hungry
   There's nobody to tell.

She sweeps her musty lodging
   As the dawn steals near,
And even if she's dead
   There's nobody to hear.

I haven't seen my neighbour
   Since a long time ago,
And even if she's dead
   There's nobody to know.

FRANCES PARK

30 Jamaica Market

Honey, pepper, leaf-green limes,
Pagan fruit whose names are rhymes,
Mangoes, breadfruit, ginger-roots,
Granadillas, bamboo-shoots,
Cho-cho, ackees, tangerines,
Lemons, purple Congo-beans,
Sugar, akras, kola-nuts,
Citrons, hairy coconuts,
Fish, tobacco, native hats,
Gold bananas, woven mats,
Plantains, wild-thyme, pallid leeks,
Pigeons with their scarlet beaks,
Oranges and saffron yams,
Baskets, ruby guava jams,
Turtles, goat skins, cinnamon,
Allspice, conch-shells, golden rum.
Black skins, babel—and the sun
That burns all colours into one.

AGNES MAXWELL-HALL

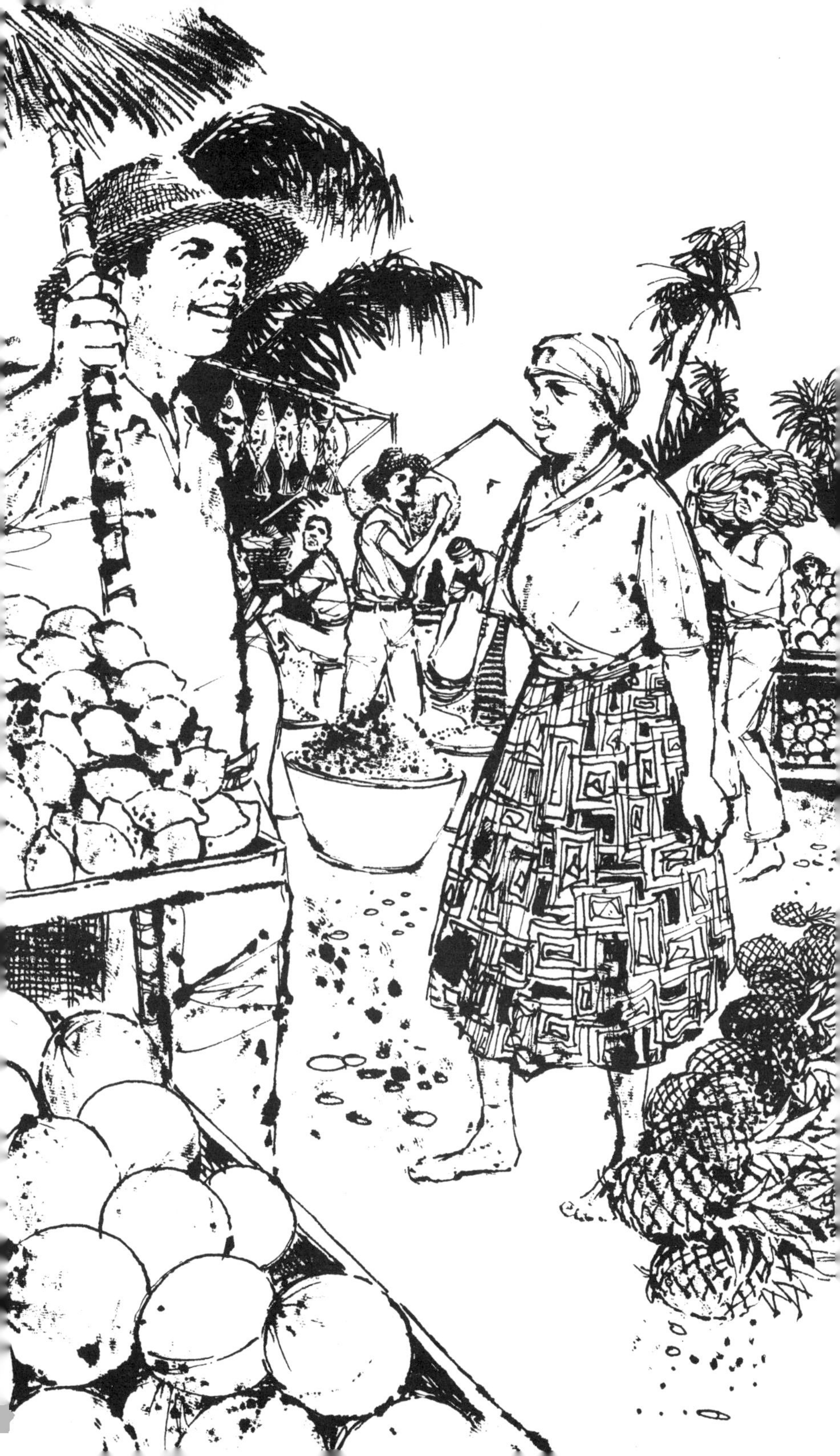

31 A Great Fast Bowler

Bowler John had to be seen to be believed. The whole of a powerful physique and a still more powerful temperament had been educated and moulded by the discipline required to hurl a batsman out and the result was a rare if not unique human being. Other bowlers can be qualified as hostile. John was not hostile, he was hostility itself. If he had been an Italian of the Middle Ages he would have been called Furioso. He had an intimidating habit of following down after the delivery if the ball was played behind the wicket. When his blood was really up he would be waiting to receive it only a few yards from you. A more striking feature of his routine was his walk back to his starting point. At the end of the day he strode back like a man just beginning. Almost every ball he was rolling up his sleeves like a man about to commit some long-premeditated act of violence. He was not the captain of his side, but I never saw his captain take him off. John always took himself off. If two batsmen made a stand against him John bowled until he broke it. Then he would take a rest, never before. The only sign of pressure was his taking a few deep breaths as he walked to his place at the end of an over. In between he did not seem to need air. Like the whale doing its business in great waters, he came up to breathe periodically. In a North v. South match during the middle twenties he had been overbowled all one day and it had become obvious that the man to get out the South was young Ellis Achong. This was agreed upon before the second day's play began. When the team walked on to the field John went up to the umpire, took the ball, and measured out his run. Though the North captain was a member of the Queen's Park Club, one of John's employers and a famous cricketer besides, neither he nor anyone else dared to say a word to John, who was bowling the match away. So can a strong man's dedication subdue all around him. He was head groundsman of the Queen's Park Oval and he ruled there like a dictator. Once they actually had to fire him. But I believe they took him back again. He belonged to the Oval and the Oval belonged to him.

In the 1923 tour he was for one reason or another left out of some matches, in his opinion unjustly. He went and sat in a remote corner of the pavilion, ostentatiously avoiding his fellow West Indians, gloomily resentful, like Achilles in his tent. After a day or two of this Austin sent one of the senior members of the team to him. "John, you don't seem very pleased with things." John (he told me this himself) replied, "What you complainin' about? I haven't said nothin' to nobody."

"Yes—but your face—"

John cut him short. "My face is my own and I'll do what I like with it."

When John was routed everybody talked of it, as people must have talked of Napoleon's defeats. He got into an argument with another intercolonial fast bowler named Lucas, at that time a man who had not played cricket for ten years. John's only argument was that Lucas was a has-been. Lucas therefore challenged him to a single-wicket match. Money was staked and ten of us agreed to field. John won the toss and batted first. He was not a bad batsman, he could hit hard and straight and he could cut, but he batted only because otherwise he would not have been able to bowl. This day the creaking Lucas bowled him a medium-paced off-break. John played and missed, the ball hit his pads and cannoned into the wicket. John had been dismissed for a duck. He rolled up his sleeves and sent down a terrible

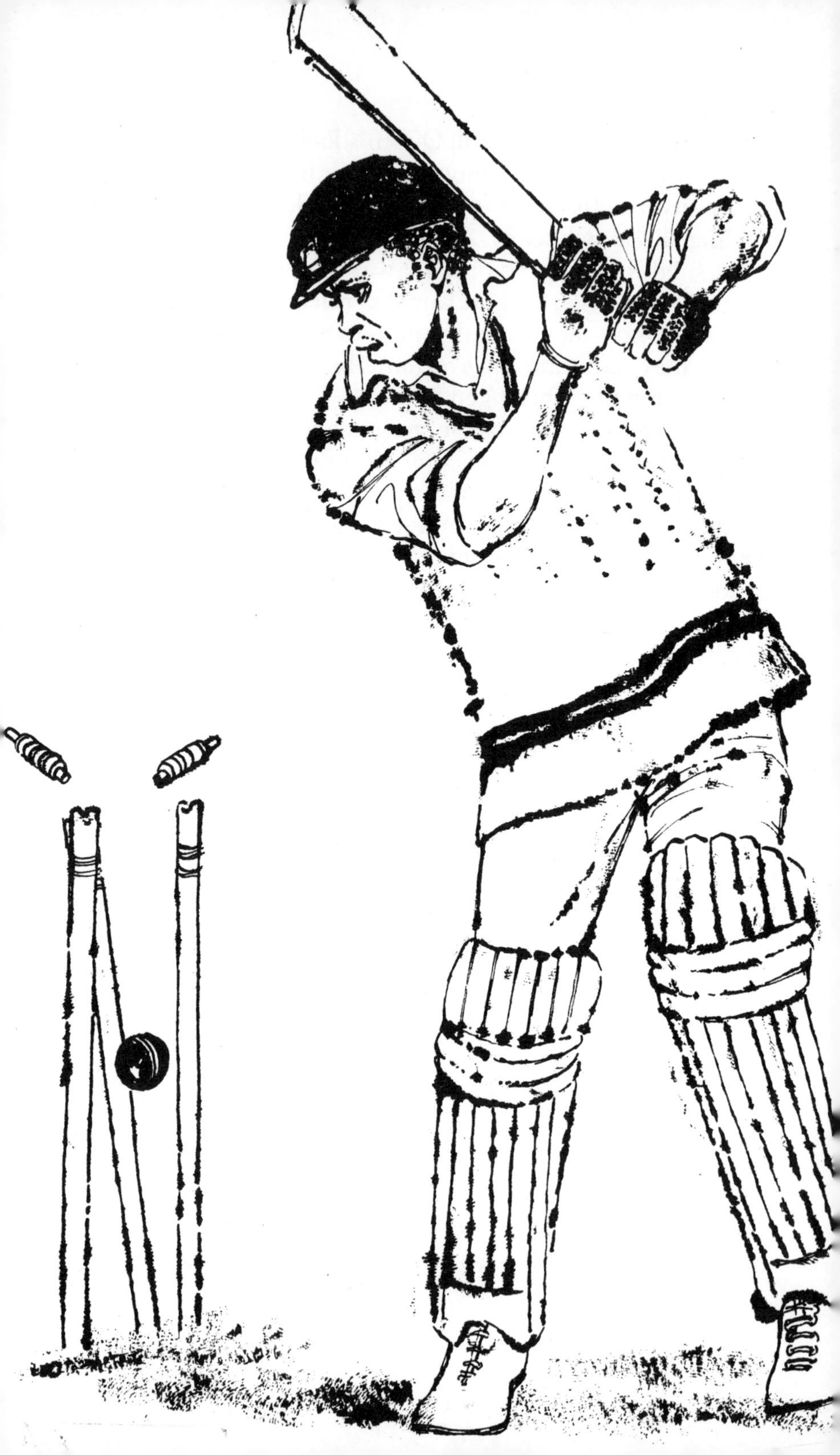

ball at Lucas. Lucas pushed out blindly, edged it for a single and John was beaten. The whole thing took two minutes. At moments like this you looked at John in a sort of terror, as if he were going to do something dreadful. He never did. I have seen him scowl at umpires, and grumble to himself, never anything else. I have never known him to get into any fight either on or off the field. Strangest of all, in the whirling of time I have never seen this fierce and formidable man bowl a short ball aimed at a batsman's head, now dignified by the euphemism of bumper. His mentality was organised around the wicket, not the player.

One afternoon at a scratch match Joe Small lifted his 2 lb 10 oz bat and drove a half-volley so hard at John's feet that he had to skip out of the way. John bowled a faster one and Small made him skip out of the way again. It was near the end of play and what did we do? As soon as play was over we hurried over to walk in with the players just to see John's face. It was a spectacle. He wasn't saying nothing to nobody and his face was his own. Long after Joe told me that he hit those balls purposely back at John's feet to make him skip: he knew it would get him mad.

Yet he had his inner discipline, and it had been hard-earned. He described to me how he had beaten a great batsman all over the place only to see an easy catch dropped in the slips.

"I suppose you were mad as hell, John."

"Me!" he said solemnly: "Not me! When that happen to you, you have to say, 'Don't mind that, old chap,' and go on bowling as if nothing happened."

It was as if he had quoted a line of Virgil to me. He must have sensed my surprise.

"No," he continued, "you have to forget it at once, for if you don't it will stay inside and upset your bowling for the rest of the day."

He had arrived at it by a road different from mine, but he had learned it well. This discipline, however, he reserved strictly for great occasions. In club games he did not disguise his always tempestuous feelings.

For some reason or other he hated Cyl St Hill, the tall left-hander, and, in any case, he was always panting to dismiss the whole Shannon crew for nothing. I do him an injustice. John was always ready to bowl out any side for nought, preferably taking all ten wickets himself. This day he was bowling like the avenging angel, and had routed the powerful Shannon side, nine for about 38 (all nine to John), when Cyl, last man in, a tall and very strong man. He was also a very determined one, and in all cricket, big as well as small, a little determination goes a long way. Cyl too was the type to say exactly what he thought of John, preferably in John's hearing.

First ball Cyl lashed out, the ball spooned up forty feet over the wicket and John had had all ten Shannon wickets, except that the wicket-keeper dropped the catch. Then came twenty glorious minutes. Cyl drove John through the covers to the boundary, a low humming hit. It was breast-high, but if you can hit hard enough there is a lot of room between gully and cover. He drove high and he drove low. He drove John straight back. When John shortened he cut him over the slips, but so hard that third man didn't bother to move. He hit him for a towering six to long-on, not too wide either. One or two went where they were not intended, but Cyl made as many as all the rest put together and Shannon, the invincible Shannon, finally reached seventy or eighty. Worst of all, I don't think John got the last wicket. When it fell he unrolled his sleeve and walked away as if he would never stop walking until he walked into the sea. Don't think he was defeated. Not he. He would put that away in his mind, and if you knew him well, and were wise enough to go to see him

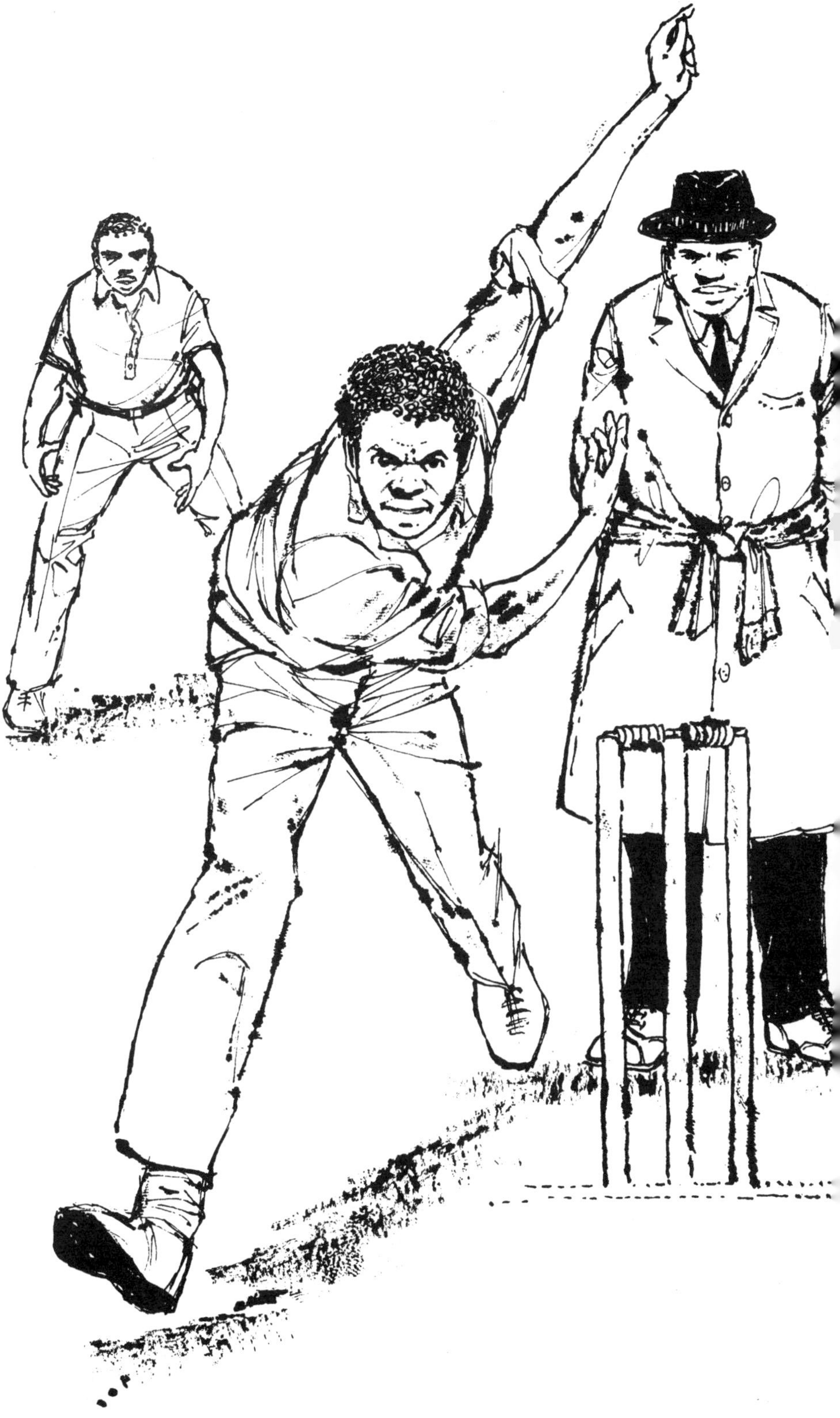

playing Shannon the following year, you would probably see Cyl bowled first ball for a duck, or his wicket shaved with a ball that only the skill of his famous brother could deal with so early in an innings.

John was one cause why I foreswore umpiring, which I loved for the close view it gave. In a trial match one afternoon he bowled a ball to Dewhurst, who played back to it. The ball hit the pad and John appealed. Before I could say anything Dewhurst's bat caught up with the ball, played it away to cover and the batsmen ran. John appealed again. I said, "Not out." He glared at me and at the end of the over remarked to whoever was near, "Some people think they know a lot about cricket, but as soon as something out of the way happen' they can't see it!" "You had to be sharp to see that one," etc. I paid no attention to him.

Then minutes afterwards he said to me, "That one was too fast for you. He was out before he hit the ball." This was John's idea of a peace-offering. I was having none of it. "You mean the ball hit his foot before he played it," I replied. "But he was not out. The ball pitched outside the off-stump." He looked daggers at me and wouldn't speak to me for the rest of the afternoon. I was on tenterhooks. Suppose there was another appeal. John would not protest or do anything out of the way. I had never known him to do that. But he would be angry, angry without compromise, and a man who can get uncompromisingly angry is one of the most effective works of God. I just didn't wish to get in the way of John's cricketing anger. In any other sphere of life I would simply have ignored him, but his cricket drew me like a magnet and in his complete dedication and disregard of all consequences I saw something of the quality which made the tragic hero, except that in John there was no tragic flaw. He was flawlessly intent on getting the batsman out and when anything went wrong he was flawlessly angry. I decided not to umpire when he was bowling. A few days after, we met and talked cricket as usual. I was a little apprehensive until I saw that he had forgotten the incident.

from BEYOND A BOUNDARY
by C. L. R. JAMES

1 John often used to continue down the wicket to collect the ball a few yards from the batsmen. He also had a habit of rolling up his sleeves while returning to his mark. What effect might these actions have had on a batsman?
2 How did John treat a dropped catch, and why?
3 John felt that Lucas was a 'has-been'. What is a 'has-been'? What single word used to describe Lucas suggests that he had not played for a long time?
4 'John . . . was bowling the match away'. Explain what this means.
5 Say whether the following sentences are true or false:
 (a) John played for a team called Shannon.
 (b) When John was angry he would bowl bouncers.
 (c) John never said anything to anybody.
 (d) John was a strong man who did not tire easily.

32   What? Protect a Hawk?

Milo and his gang were in a fix. That smart aleck Jim had done the impossible—caught the hawk that had for so long eluded everybody else. He had passed the test of fire, proved himself the best. And yet—yet he could not be, could never be allowed into the club. They had to do something. They either had to set the hawk free, or else kidnap the bird. They'd prefer to set him free, but Jim was right: the bird wouldn't stand a chance out there. So they decided to snatch him and keep him in their secret clubhouse. As soon as he was well they'd set him free again, their boon sky friend.

While Jim was out hunting for food for the bird the three boys crept up on his home. It did not take long for them to discover the whereabouts of the hawk, for Mr Big immediately proclaimed his presence in the garage, flapping his wings and *caw*ing and *piyaah*ing.

"Let's go get him," Mule whispered.

"We'll have to be smarter than that," Milo said. "We'll come back in the night and take him. 'Twill be so easy."

"Right," agreed Mongoose.

"We'll come back tonight and take that hawk," Milo reaffirmed.

As they emerged from the bush Mrs Anderson saw them from the window. She did not like their rough appearance, but, believing they were simply taking a shortcut to the road, she gave no thought to the hawk. She wondered if the boys knew Jim and if this allowed them to feel free to come so close to the house.

Jim returned with three birds, two lapwings and a dove. By his reckoning, they weighed a good pound and a half together, enough, he thought, for Mr Big. Maybe hawks did not care for such birds, having gotten to like sophisticated chicken meat, but as far as Jim was concerned Mr Big was in a hospital, and when people go to hospital they can't be too choosey. The hawk would have to eat whatever he brought.

He plucked out the feathers and dropped a bird into the cage. The hawk reacted instantly. But Jim noticed that he was having difficulty balancing himself on his injured leg while he held his food in the good one as he tore the meat off with his beak.

"I know how to fix that, Mr Big," he said softly.

He cut the remaining birds into small bits. The hawk eagerly devoured the food and seemed to appreciate the gesture.

Jim went into the house and found his mother at her sewing machine. He told her how he had provided food for the hawk, assuring her that it would be no problem to feed him for a couple of weeks.

"Some boys were about," she said casually, her foot pedalling the machine.

"Some boys?" asked Jim quickly.

"Maybe looking for you?"

"What did they look like, Mom?"

His mother described them.

"Milo and his friends," he murmured. "What were they doing, ma'am?"

"Oh, I don't know, Jim. Seems to me they were returning to the village. But, say, what is it?"

"Oh, I don't know ma'am. But it seems funny to me. We are not exactly friends."

"Oh?"

Jim told her the whole story, how they had taken his marbles, then set him the test of catching the hawk alive. He related how they had stalled in initiating him into their club. "Mom, you know what I think? There's something phoney or crooked about those boys."

"What d'you mean exactly, Jim?"

"I think they're after Mr Big."

"Why?"

"Maybe to kill him and take the credit."

"Yes, yes, I can see that they might."

"I'd better bring him into the house."

"The hawk? Jim Anderson, are you off your rocker? A canary yes, or a pigeon. But a hawk in the house? Good Lord, no, no, no. Over my dead body, no!"

"But, Mom, I can't see him stolen and butchered like that. It's not sporting."

"Wait for your father."

"Yes, ma'am."

When Jim heard the car coming up the hill he went out to meet his father. He wanted to be the one to break the news.

"Hi, Dad," he called as his father alighted from the car, straightening his back.

"And how're you doing, Jim?"

"Fine, Dad, real good. You know Kendal's not a bad place after all."

"You don't say. Coming from you, that's a big change, Jim." He reached into the car and brought out his lunch pail. Jim snatched it from his hand and carried it.

"What happened today, Jim?"

Jim let it fall like a brick. "I caught a hawk."

"Hawk, hawk, hawk. . . . The kind that flies?"

"The kind that flies, sir."

"And preys on birds and chickens as well?"

"That's the kind, Dad."

His dad swallowed. "What did you shoot him with?

Jim laughed. "He's alive, Dad. I tricked him. You see."

"Jim, you humour me, boyo."

"It's true, Dad. Come and see." He led his father into the garage.

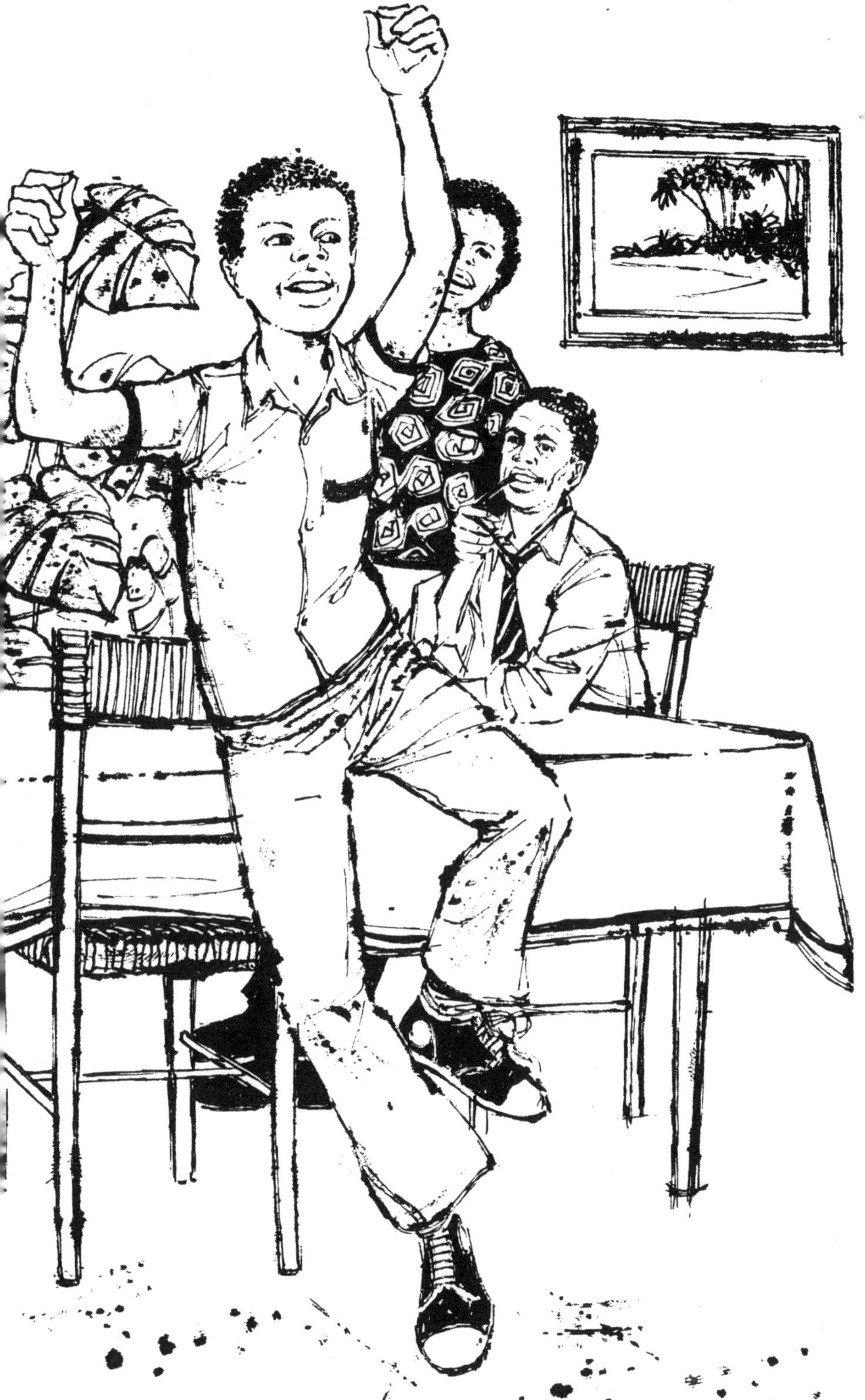

When Mr Anderson saw the hawk his eyes boggled. "And he's so big! How'd you do it? Well, I'll be, Jim —" he said finally.

At supper Mr Anderson was filled in on the details as he ate. He listened without interrupting the story.

"You do have a problem, Jim boyo," he then said. "Know what I mean?"

"Yes sir."

"There's the trouble of keeping him fed—"

"I killed three birds for him today."

"Yes, yes. But you were free all day. I mean—what happens on a school day? And will your luck always hold, boyo?"

Jim said nothing. He could see his father's logic.

"Not likely, son," his father went on. "So you can't keep him. Yet you can't release him—not yet, not while he's injured. He wouldn't stand a bird of a chance out there." He rubbed his chin thoughtfully. "So I guess you'll have to keep him until he's well."

"Hooray!" Jim shouted, dancing around the table.

"Don't rejoice as yet, boyo. That too might be a stiff problem. Just supposing that hawk gets to kind of like you. What then? He'll want to stay on. There are two things bad about that. One—you'll tend to continue taking care of him and liking him more and more. And number two—it'd be so much easier for him to be shot, being kind of—shall we say—semi-tame, boyo? And then what? There goes your heart, breaking over a dead old hawk. Then there's problem number three staring us in the face. The people—"

"That's what I told him," Mrs Anderson said as she began clearing the table.

"Yes, they're the ones. If they find out you've got him they'll want him delivered for what's coming. And they'd be right."

"Do I have to, Dad? Deliver him?"

"I'm not for a live hawk around here, boyo, but neither can I see him delivered up to be killed just—just like that."

"Just as I thought. I read you right," Jim said.

"What we have to do," Mr Anderson continued, "is to get him well, then release him. Not around here. We'll drive far out into the countryside to do it. And if he gets killed, at least he'll have been given his chance."

"Hooray!" said Jim, dancing another jig. "Thanks Dad. Mom, you know you married the right man."

They smiled at him, then at each other, and his mother held her hand up in a victory sign.

"But we have to keep it quiet," Mr Anderson said.

Jim and his mother exchanged glances. "Oh-oh," said Jim. "We can't keep it quiet, Dad."

"Why not?"

Jim told him about the Milo affair.

"Too bad," he said. "It makes the job much harder, but we'll see."

"Dad, you're a plus."

And so, with Mr Anderson's approval, Mr Big was brought into the house.

from BABA AND MR BIG
by C. EVERARD PALMER

1 What do you think is meant by 'the bird wouldn't stand a chance out there'? Why did the boy think so?
2 What is meant by 'off your rocker'? Why did Jim's mother say this?
3 What problems did Jim's father see in keeping the hawk?
4 Try to give a reason why 'Milo and his gang were in a fix'.
5 Relate a story about wanting to keep something that your parents did not like. What happened?

Nelson's New West Indian Readers

A six-year reading course specially prepared to meet the needs of primary teachers in the Caribbean.

Throughout the course particular attention is paid to the selection of structural items and vocabulary. The structures in the first books are those that are often misused, so that by constantly reading and repeating them, children will be able to overcome their difficulties.

Infant Books 1 and 2
Clive Borely
These provide the child with the phonic skills necessary to translate written symbols into speech. Complete sentences are used from the start so that the child's task is challenging and meaningful. Full colour illustrations throughout.

Infant Story Books
Additional reading material to accompany the Infant Books:
Spot and Tippy
A Day at the Sea
A Day on the Farm
Looking after Tim

Infant Workbooks
Clive Borely
These workbooks provide exercises and pictures which help the child to discover and use certain phonic rules. Once the tests have been completed the children can colour in the illustrations themselves.
Infant Workbook 1
Infant Workbook 2

Introductory Books 1 and 2
Clive Borely
A continuation of the Infant Books, containing simple stories about situations and events that are familiar to Caribbean children.

Introductory Workbooks
Clive Borely
Two more workbooks, to accompany the Introductory Books, in the same format as the new Infant Workbooks.
Introductory Workbook 1
Introductory Workbook 2

Books 1–5
Stories and poems followed by exercises, with many stories about the Caribbean.

Book 1 *Undine Giuseppi*
Book 2 *Undine Giuseppi*
Book 3 *Gordon Bell*
Book 4 *Undine Giuseppi*
Book 5 *Clive Borely*

Workbooks for Books 1 and 2
Undine Giuseppi
Four workbooks to accompany Books 1 and 2.